From This Day Forward

Switched at Marriage, Episode 4

Gina Robinson

Gina Robinson
SEATTLE, WASHINGTON

From This Day Forward, Switched at Marriage 4/ Gina Robinson. — 1st ed.
ISBN 978-0692473740

For Jeff

CONTEMPORARY ROMANCE
ECHO BAY CHRISTMAS

CHAPTER ONE

Kayla

When facing one of life's universal dilemmas—whether to open Pandora's box or calmly go on with life as if nothing extraordinary has happened—you should always listen to the tiny voice of reason in your head. Your conscience will be your guide—

Right. That's something my mom would say. I wanted her out of my head. *Now.*

The envelope I'd found in Justin's coat pocket shook in my hand as I studied his neat, engineering block printing.

To my Wife Kayla, to be read the day before our divorce.

I plopped down on the padded black bench in Justin's rather ordinary closet and set the coat beside me.

His closet *should* have been fabulous. I mean, it *was* a billionaire's closet. Or pretending to be, anyway. In a penthouse. And huge. At least half the size of my entire apartment. But sparse. Definitely thin on shelves. Racks for shoes? Nearly nonexistent. He had *a* shelf for shoes. Yes, *one* tiny shelf. Who had so few shoes that one shelf would hold them?

Even before being a billionaire's wife, I'd fantasized about a closet with wall-to-wall shoes, neatly laid out in custom shoe shelf after custom shelf. Filled with fabulous designer shoes. As a nearly starving college grad I had more shoes than would fit on that shelf. If I had it entirely to myself.

He also had shelves for his jeans. Which might have been a practical storage solution if he'd owned *hundreds* of pairs, not a mere half dozen. Neatly folded and sitting side by side. The man *needed* more clothes. As in way, *way* more! How was he going to compete with Lazer with this shoddy wardrobe?

From the look of his closet layout, he wasn't planning on buying many more. Good thing I was riding to his fashion rescue. If I was going to leave him as the smokingly hottest divorced billionaire in the city in less than a year, I had no time to lose. Not even one of his precious computing nanoseconds. How small was a nanosecond, anyway?

Either Jus had cheaped out on closet design. Or he'd hired a minimalist to design it. It was like his old college clothes were lounging in the luxury of empty space. That was what all the money in the world meant to Jus, more space for the meager wardrobe he already had. A closet this big should have had plenty of room for me to move into. But it needed a California Closet makeover, like, immediately. I was going to talk to Jus about it. The next woman in his life would thank me. Why did the thought of handing all my hard work over to another girl give me a prickle of jealousy?

I shrugged it off as nothing more than wanting to get credit for a job well done. Which brought me back to the matter at hand.

Hmmmm...the day before our divorce? What was *so* special about immediately before the dissolution of our marriage?

I turned the envelope over, caressing the fine quality paper as if I could seduce it into giving up the secrets within. What could Jus *possibly* have to say to me that *had* to wait until the day before our scheduled divorce? The possibilities certainly piqued my imagination.

My vanity reveled in the idea that he was madly in love with me and was going to beg me to stay. Yes, I was a wicked woman that way, wanting male adoration forever. But weren't we all to some degree? And the thought, while sweet and romantic, was preposterous. College crushes didn't last forever. And he'd made no move to give me any indication his feelings were as they had been. Which had been immature and naïve at best, anyway.

However, if he were going to beg me to stay, he would have to at least promise me a major closet over-haul. With plenty of shelves for shoes and drawers for fine lingerie. And at least a tiny bit of femininity in the décor. Enough of this black, red, and gray.

Or...

He was handing down sage investing advice. Maybe the name of a trusted financial advisor, and in the card was a brilliant letter of introduction. Because this financial advisor was so exclusive and hard to get I would need a referral. I had no experience managing real money. And Jus was sweet enough to take care of me even when I was no longer "his responsibility." I laughed at that thought. But he wouldn't want me blowing that hard-earned ten million he was forking over.

Or...

The card contained a letter of recommendation to the next billionaire, or maybe even only multimillionaire, who needed a decoy wife. Yes, a reference like you'd give a nanny when her charges had outgrown the need for her services. *Is fiercely loyal and discreet. Can be trusted not to blow your cover. Sometimes gets carried away and flirts with other men. But will treat your mother with respect and can be reminded of her duty to be in love with you. At least in public.*

And, hey, maybe after a year, when I earned my gold digger's green card, I would be in the mood to make a career out of decoy wifery. I might even prove to have a real aptitude for it.

Or...

The card contained a press release announcing our divorce and the "reasons" for it. The official party line, so to speak. And a reminder that either I took this secret to my grave, or Jus would destroy me with his superior mind and computer hacking skills.

Or...

He was giving me instructions on where to leave my keys to his many homes, all the credit cards in our names, and any other logistical details of parting ways. Wait. Couldn't Handsome Harry handle all that?

Sigh. I could go on and on. The possibilities were endless.

But why should I when I could simply open the envelope? Read what he had to say. Toss the card in the trash in the lobby. And donate the coat as planned. He would *never know the difference*. So easy, really.

I grinned. Child's play. I was about to slip my finger beneath the envelope's flap when the chime of the alarm system sounded. Not the ear-splitting siren of the alarm actually going off. The alarm wasn't armed. The pleasant warning bing-bong that alerted me that a door had opened. Either Magda, or the part-time maid, was working on Saturday. Or...

"Kay! I'm home. Where are you?"

Crappity, crap, crap! Justin was home. *Early*. Such unfortunate timing.

I sat with my back to the closet entrance. I was looking around for a place to stash the letter—

"There you are!"

I jumped. Nearly out of my skin, as they say. And now I knew why.

"Caught you red-handed!" His footsteps came toward me.

My mouth went cotton dry as I tried to think like a spy. How could he have caught me? Did he have cameras in the closet?

I didn't have time to eat the evidence. And no saliva to swallow it if I had. I almost gave up and simply handed the letter over to him. But I wasn't a quitter.

"What are you doing in here?" His voice grew louder as he grew closer.

So maybe he didn't mean he'd caught me with his card. Cool as Mata Hari, I slipped the envelope back into the jacket pocket to retrieve later and fixed a welcoming, totally innocent smile on my lips. "Conquering your *horrendous* closet. And making room to infiltrate your life. What else would I be doing in here?"

So innocent and flippant! I sounded completely normal despite my wildly racing heart.

He rested his hands on my shoulders and leaned down to whisper in my ear. "Do you have a flag?"

"What?" I laughed. He was ridiculous sometimes. And obscure.

"You can't claim new territory without a flag. No flag, no closet."

I scooped a pair of panties off the floor and waved them for effect. "How's this?"

"Like waving a red flag in front of a bull."

I glanced up at him. His comment caught me off guard. Was he really interested in sex? He'd been so damned gentlemanly. I wasn't used to men who kept it in their pockets.

"More like bullshit," I said. "Since when have you been a raging bull?" I laughed.

A quick look of hurt flashed across his face so quickly I almost missed it. I'd hurt his masculine pride, I suppose. He was too complex for me to figure out sometimes.

I cleared my throat and tried to appear apologetic. "Besides, they're black."

"Flying the black flag? Even worse." He rubbed my shoulders, back to sounding friendly and uninterested.

I hoped he didn't feel how tense and knotted I was. His hands were working magic. "You plagiarized that joke. You stole it from an old comedy routine you played for me in college. Don't think I don't know your MO."

He shook his head. "I modified it to suit the situation. That's not plagiarism. That's putting a fresh spin on old material." His hands stilled. With one quick movement, he pulled his jacket out of my hand before I could protest. "Great! You found my jacket. I went off without it this morning."

"You can't take that!" I wanted it. And most importantly, I wanted that tantalizing letter back.

"I just did."

"Toss it over there," I said, as casually as I could. As if I wasn't dying to get it back. "In the donation pile. I'll have Magda take all that stuff to the Goodwill on Monday."

"No way, baby," he whispered in my ear. "This is my favorite. You're giving my good stuff away?"

"I'm giving your crap stuff away. To make room for a few of my clothes. Like enough to last a year. So I don't look like a temporary visitor. Or a slob who keeps her clothes on a chair because she's too lazy to put them away." I patted the seat next to me. "Has anyone ever told you this closet is just an excuse to waste space? Where are all the fabulous shelves and drawers like a billionaire should have? I need shelves and drawers for my things."

"So order some," he said in a tone of totally not caring about either the money or the details of a closet as he took the seat I offered. "I've only been a billionaire about a month. What with Flash going public, becoming a billionaire, and taking a wife, I'm not up on how billionaires' closets should look yet. Is there some standard? An international code of billionaires' closets I should be following? Or is this another one of those social conventions I'm blind to?"

I laughed. He was sweet. And funny. And honest.

"Codes? Not that I'm aware of. Social conventions, probably. Leave it to me. I'll take care of it and get you up to code and social convention standards. Straight away." I glanced around the closet and pursed my mouth. "I really don't know why this master suite doesn't have his and hers closets, anyway."

"This penthouse was billed as a bachelor pad." He sounded amused. "That was its appeal in the first place. I wasn't thinking of getting married when I bought it. I don't plan to live here forever."

I turned and rolled my eyes at him. "Oh, baby, you really blew the bachelor bit."

He nodded. "What can I say? I have no defense."

I patted his hand and smiled into his eyes. "One of these days I'm going to have to check 'our' other homes and see if one is more suited for family life."

"Don't get your hopes up. The other homes are nice, but I like this place." He grinned devilishly.

My heart did the tiniest flop as he did. He had an intense way of looking at me, maybe at any girl, really, like he was interested and really saw me.

"So only your needs matter in this marriage?" I grinned back, teasing him. It was so easy and natural. "*I* could always move into one of them. We could live separate lives like so many jet-setting couples."

Talking had put him off guard.

I saw a chance and made a sudden move to take back his jacket. "Give me that ratty thing! I'm on a mission to give it away to someone who's desperate enough to actually need to wear it."

He dodged my attempt to gain control of the jacket, laughing. "Nice try. As long as I'm paying for your services as my wife, you stay with me. And so does this jacket."

I rolled my eyes. "You're impossible! And although I fear I've set feminism back a hundred years with this marriage of convenience and fakery, I never promised to obey you." I sighed for dramatic emphasis, obviously still teasing him.

"You signed a contract. With the terms spelled out. That's even better." He laughed again. "Speaking of our marriage, how am I supposed to act at this party tonight? Cool and aloof? Like an arrogant, cocky douchebag billionaire snob? So when we split in a year your friends will side with you. I don't want to get this wrong again and end up in the doghouse. It's damn tight in there and my allergies act up."

His tone was light and joking. But comedy usually hides darkness and hurt. I had the feeling he still stung from my—and I will say it—seemingly irrational reaction to how much my parents liked him. It was odd. They've never particularly liked any of my previous boyfriends. Although by previous, that pretty much meant Eric, for the most part. So maybe that's why I was upset. They didn't like the guys I picked and loved the one I didn't.

"I blew it with your parents. I don't want to get in trouble again. So? Do you want me to hide my natural charm?" Jus gave me a sweet smile, seductive in its earnestness.

When had Eric cared about my feelings? The thought came out of nowhere. I realized I hadn't thought much about Eric at all during the first week of my marriage. And my heart was feeling considerably less bruised. It hardly hurt at all.

"Just so you know," Jus continued, "I have *not* sent flowers ahead this time."

My turn to raise an eyebrow at him. "Champagne?"

"Nope."

"A fruit basket?"

He rolled his eyes.

"Chocolate-covered strawberries?"

"No way."

"Excellent!" I hugged him and looked deep into his eyes, touched by how much he wanted to please me. "How sweet and unthoughtful you are."

"Yeah, I'm now that kind of guy. The kind who doesn't do thoughtful shit. So?"

His point hit home. Crap, I *was* being that confusing kind of girl guys hated. That I hated, too, come to think of it. I wasn't intentionally jerking him around on my string. This whole situation confused and confounded me, too.

On the surface, I may have looked like the socially savvy one. But being in a marriage of convenience was way more complicated than I ever could have imagined. Like so many things in life, you don't know what you're getting into until you dive in. If I didn't know what I wanted, how could he? Even mind reading wouldn't have helped him in this situation, sad to say. Not that I'm in favor of mind reading. I didn't like the thought of someone knowing my thoughts.

"I'm sorry." I flashed him a genuinely contrite and apologetic smile. "Who knew fake wives could be such absolute bitches and pains in the ass, right?"

He laughed. "Kay—"

I shook my head. "No, it's okay. It's true. I never thought I'd be a bitchy, confusing, controlling, demanding wife. I always pictured myself as a mature, sensible, loving kind of partner." I took a breath. "I'm feeling my way through this. It's uncharted territory for me." I shook my head and laughed softly. "For anybody, I suppose. How many marriages like ours are there?"

"Statistically speaking?" His eyes were full of humor. "Disregarding all the standard marriages of convenience, you know, where they actually get married." His grin was adorable.

I couldn't help smiling. It surprised me, really, how easily he made me smile. He had an infectious good humor and sweetness. Had Eric done that for me? Certainly not in the last year, maybe longer. In the beginning, yes. Due to sheer infatuation and the happy hormones involved in falling in love. But how long had that lasted until the betrayal and the fighting and the off-and-on started?

"And all green card marriages, arranged marriages, and out-and-out scam marriages," Jus said, continuing with the theme, "I'd say we're at least one in a million."

"I'd say that's generous." I smiled at him, feeling lighter. "I was thinking one in a billion."

"It's all right, Kay. I don't mind if you're a bitch from time to time. There's no road map for what we're going through." He took a deep breath, like he was bracing for something. "Look. You hung by me in college when everyone else ostracized and made fun of me. You treated me like a normal guy. Not a joke. Not a scrawny kid who didn't belong anywhere. I can certainly put up with a little confusion on your part in a crazy situation like this one that *I* dragged you into." He winked. "Even if I am paying you to play the part. I give all my employees a trial time to learn the job. A wise boss doesn't expect perfection from the start."

My eyes misted. Crap, he *was* sweet. Thoughtful. Considerate. And maybe, best off all, reasonable.

I swallowed a lump that was fast forming in my throat. "I wasn't *that* nice."

"Nice enough that I developed a mad crush on you."

I looked into his eyes, startled that he'd brought it up. "You're just into older women, that's all. And I was convenient."

I could have bit my lip. I had a habit of brushing heartfelt compliments aside as if they were nothing. I didn't know why I couldn't just smile and accept them. They made me uncomfortable, I guess. Deep down, I felt I didn't deserve them. I was a little embarrassed. Because, really, I hadn't been *that* nice.

I'd known he had a crush on me. And though I'd defended him in public, and tried to put a stop to it when my sorority sisters teased me about it, I never considered him boyfriend material. I felt, and yes, this is hard to admit, but we've all felt it at one time or another, that he was beneath me. Now, it seemed superficial. And silly. Here he was, not even twenty-two and one of the most important, and richest, men in the city.

So no, I didn't really deserve that compliment. But that he admitted that crush so openly, and vulnerably, now, was more than sort of adorable.

He laughed. "You weren't unique because you were older than me. *Everyone* was older than I was. Even the high school seniors who came to campus on college visits." He laughed, more at himself than anything. "You don't give yourself enough credit, Kay. You treated me like a person, not a freak. Very few people did. Especially cool, popular people like you were."

I almost corrected him and told him I wasn't *that* popular *or* cool. Just insecure enough to try to be. I caught myself just in time. "That's sweet. Really. Flattering."

He shook his head. "You're too nice. There's no need to lie. I was an immature geek then. Still am in many ways."

"No." I shook my head.

He raised one eyebrow.

I laughed. "Well, maybe. Maybe we both were. I was so *stupidly* infatuated with Eric." I was surprised by how put out I sounded, and felt, about my stupid younger self, as in an entire week younger, wasting so much time on him.

Jus winced. "Sorry. Didn't mean to bring up a sore subject."

"Sore subject?" I snorted softly, my favored sound of derision. "Is that what he is?"

"He's not one of *my* favorite topics." He glanced down at his feet. "Even a husband of convenience doesn't like to think of his new bride longing for an ex."

"I'm not longing for him." The words popped out of my mouth without thought. But I realized with a start that they were true.

He glanced up from his feet to me with a skeptical look on his face.

"Honestly." I put my hand lightly on Justin's arm. It was warm and hard beneath my touch. And maybe it was my imagination, but I thought his breath caught a little.

"Oh, sure, I like the revenge of marrying up, way out of his league." I smiled softly at Jus, a swell of pride rising deep within. "He'll *never* accomplish anything near what you have. No, I've barely thought of him all week." I paused. "You make me forget all about him, my dearest husband of wild fakery."

He shook his head, but his grin was way too wide.

"Jus?" I rested my hands at either side of me and gripped the padded bench I sat on. My heart raced as a question formed on my lips.

"Yeah?" He mimicked my pose. Our hands were so close they nearly touched.

I was actually, surprisingly, tempted to loop my pinkie around his. "Why a year?"

He frowned ever so slightly. "Why a year what?"

"For this marriage." I held his gaze. "Why not six months? Or three years? Or a decade? I get why not a few days or weeks. But what's magic about a year?"

He didn't answer. So I pressed him. "Is there a secret will I should know about? Like a long-lost aunt passed away leaving you another few billions. But only if you marry and stay married for a year? Otherwise, all the money goes to her eighteen cats? Because, you know, you could tell me that. Though I might ask for a bigger piece of the pie if that's the case. Saving a fortune from cats is hard work, after all."

"There's no secret will." His eyes sparkled. He was clearly amused.

"So you could end this early? *If* you wanted to." The thought just occurred to me.

"I suppose." He shrugged. "If I wanted to. But." He took a deep breath, like he was bracing to give a long-winded explanation. "Don't get your hopes of collecting that ten million early just yet. I really do need the time to make sure the ID thief can't hurt us or Flash." He paused. Started to speak. And stopped himself.

"What?" My heart pounded in my ears. "What's happened?"

"She texted me." He whipped out his phone and showed me the text.

"The girl on the news is not the Kayla Green you married," I real aloud, before turning my gaze to his. I stared at him with wide eyes.

"It's from a burner phone," he said. "Untraceable."

"That text is from days ago." I swallowed, thinking hard and fast. "Why didn't you tell me?"

"I didn't want to worry you. She's my problem. I'll deal with her. I gave myself a year, right from the start, to make sure she can't cause problems."

"It's *our* problem now." My mouth was dry. "If my family finds out I faked this marriage"—I gave him a small smile—"especially now that they've fallen in love with you—"

"They won't." He covered my hand with his. "I promise."

"Jus, you have to let me in on this. You have to keep me informed. We're a team now." I paused, afraid to ask the next question. "How did she get your number?"

He sighed. "From your phone, I assume."

I felt myself pale. "She downloaded my contact list?" The thought made me nauseated.

He shrugged. "Maybe. Or maybe she just kept my number. You know, to look up later. So she could laugh at me. Or who the hell knows what."

I turned my hand over, palm up to his, and laced my fingers through his. "Has she asked for money? Has she blackmailed you?"

His expression hardened. He clasped my hand tightly in his. "I won't give her money. Don't worry. But to answer your question, no. That's the only communication from her."

"But she has to want something—"

"She won't get it. I'll stop her." His face was fierce with determination. "I'll find her."

"And then what?"

"Just what I said before. I'll neutralize her."

I shivered. "What does that mean, exactly?" Though I wasn't sure I wanted to know.

He clutched my hand and ran his thumb over mine. His grip was amazingly comforting.

"Just what it implies—I'll fix it so she can never hurt either of us. I can do it within a year. I'm sure I can." He bumped me gently with his shoulder. "I'm sorry I had to tell you. It wasn't my intent to upset you before our wedding party. We're supposed to look like a carefree, happy couple."

"I'm glad you did. You'll tell me if she contacts you again?"

He nodded. "Promise. Now, you still haven't told me how I'm supposed to act around your friends." He grinned, dismissing the ID thief as suddenly insignificant.

"Like your charming self, of course." I smiled into his eyes. "Seriously, just be yourself and we'll be fine." And I meant it. "But it would help, in the future, if we maintain a public persona. You know, the kind of couple we are."

He arched an eyebrow and studied me. "Just what *is* our persona?"

I shrugged. "So far? I'd say sweetly in love. Stunned by the sudden passion and realization, not to mention impulsiveness, of our feelings for each other. Giddy, maybe, with the feeling of being newly in love and having found our soul mate. The public loves that kind of stuff. We should run with it."

He nodded. His eyes narrowed. "Is that what we've shown to everyone? Friends and family, too?"

"My family loves the idea of us. And your mom is coming around to me."

"Our friends? Your friends? What should *they* see?" He shot those arrows of accusation with deadly precision.

I fought back a blush as I remembered the EIEIO meeting and lunch with Britt. Maybe I had been a little too obvious with Lazer. I flashed Jus an innocent smile. "The same as everyone else—a couple very much in love."

"So that's how we play it?" His grin was adorable. "If I follow your lead will I stay out of trouble?"

I laughed and shook my head. "Maybe."

"Good enough."

My cell phone buzzed in my pocket. I pulled it out and glanced at it. Lazer had texted me. *You're in, princess! Take a look. What do you think? Spectacularly gorgeous!*

A picture of a video game princess popped up. She looked like me. Except for the overspillage of cleavage and impossibly narrow waist. I was neither that amply endowed nor that tiny in the midsection. Everything about the characterized me was enhanced. And I loved her!

Just got confirmation that you're in the alpha test group, too. In real life. I'm free this afternoon. Do you want to play a game?

I must have gotten a lovesick smile on my face.

"Lazer?" All the fun and flippancy left Justin's voice. He removed his hand from mine.

I looked up at him and tried not to appear guilty as charged. "Yeah. I've been approved to be in the alpha test for a new game he's involved in. You should ask him to get you in the group, too."

Jus shook his head. "I don't have time to play games."

But wasn't that pretty much what we were doing *all* the time?

"I'm in the game as a character, too," I said. "Isn't it awesome? How did you know?"

"Among my many talents, I can read upside down."

"A multitalented man! *Impressive.*" I handed him the phone. "See?"

His face became unreadable as he studied the texted picture. "Hot."

I laughed, self-conscious. His tone didn't exactly ooze enthusiasm. "Thank you. I think."

He handed my phone back. "Is this princess in the final, public-release version of the game?"

I frowned. "Yes, of course." I was confused. Was there any other version? "She's not a playable character, though. Why?"

Jus shrugged. "No reason. You're sure? It's common enough for game developers to make custom versions for select clients, like Lazer. I've even known guys who've proposed to their girlfriends via a custom game. They get a special 'proposal' level built in. The developers get a kick out of helping out fanatic fans."

"I assumed..." Now I wasn't sure.

"You can always ask Lazer." Jus was too casual.

He'd done a perfect job of seeding doubt in my mind. *Was* Lazer playing me? And how in the world would I ask him?

"I'm gaming with another guy." I paused and studied Jus, but his face was still a mask. "You're not jealous?"

He held my gaze. "You like Lazer? If it wasn't for our fake marriage, you'd go after him?"

Why had my mouth gone suddenly dry again? "If it wasn't for our 'marriage,' I never would have met him."

"You can be honest with me, Kay. If you like him, you like him." His tone was neutral, almost damningly unconcerned.

"I think we could have chemistry." I was suddenly defensive. It showed unintentionally in my tone. "Under different circumstances."

Jus continued studying me. "He's my mentor and one of my good friends."

"I know. I'm sorry." In my rush to apologize, I practically slurred my words together.

Jus shrugged. "That's *not* what I meant. I mean, he doesn't know this is a decoy marriage to shut that ID-thieving bitch down." His gaze was piercing.

"I haven't told him." Why did I feel the need to defend myself against an accusation he hadn't voiced?

"I didn't say you did. The point is he doesn't know. And yet he flirts with my new bride and makes a romantic gesture, like turning her into a hot video game princess."

"He's not flirting. I don't think that's how he sees it. He's just being nice—"

Jus snorted and shook his head. "Guys aren't *nice* like that, sweetheart. He's flirting. He's a player, Kay. Just like Eric. Always has been." He paused. "Or worse—he's up to something. Scheming. Be careful what you tell him. About us. About anything."

He took my hand again. "One thing you learn when you run in billionaires' circles—don't trust anyone."

CHAPTER TWO

Justin

Lazer *was* up to something, damn him. He was a lot of interesting, odd, and eclectic things, but a wife stealer wasn't one of them. That I was aware of, anyway. He had enough beautiful single women falling all over him. He didn't need to poach mine. Or anyone else's. I'd never known him to lose his heart. He jounced from one relationship to another unscathed, leaving a trail of broken, and often bitter, hearts in his wake. His, I swore, was made of impenetrable armor. It would take a woman armed with a nuclear weapon to get to him.

Even if I hadn't been in love with Kay, just out of friendliness, I would have warned her off him. Lazer wasn't the committed type.

What the hell was his game? If he was suspicious of what I was up to, I had to throw him off. It would have been nice to confide in him about the jam I was in. He was my mentor, after all. And a hell of lot smoother with the ladies than I could ever hope to be. But the fewer people who knew the truth, the better. And I wasn't certain, one hundred percent, that he wouldn't use it against me. Clichéd to say, but business was a dog-eat-dog world. And both of us were determined to be the alpha.

On impulse, I texted Lazer. *Stop flirting with my wife. I'm the guy who's supposed to make her feel like a princess.*

He texted right back. *Was I flirting? Sorry, man. I'll back off. Just thought she'd get a kick out of being in a game. No poaching intended.*

The text exchange then degenerated into a discussion about business. I didn't hold a grudge. And I didn't want to put him on guard. If nothing else in my bullied life, I'd learned the usefulness of putting your adversary at ease. I'd perfected the art of the sneak attack. In this case, I hoped I didn't have to use it.

I felt isolated and alone. In this and everything. I didn't sleep alone anymore, but I may as well have. Having Kay's hot, shapely body in the bed next to me night after night only provided temptation. And the fear of embarrassing wet dreams.

Besides, she messed with my sleep app. It recorded her body movement as well as mine. And man, was she an active sleeper! At least according to the app. I checked the data after our first night together and it was like she'd been jumping on the bed with wild abandon. I wished it meant we'd been having vigorous sex. Which, to my great frustration, I knew for a sad fact was *not* the case. It must have been a bug in the software. Kay hardly moved when she slept.

I'd had a moment of excitement, thinking the app would have recorded the movement of me and the ID thief having sex, if there had been any. The app showed nothing but the slumber of the dead. Then I remembered I'd been drugged and hadn't even gotten the phone out of my pocket that night. So, as far as legal proof, that was a no-go. At the same time, I realized sleeping with my phone didn't exactly make me look suave, anyway. I didn't need to emphasize my nerdiness. It made itself known all on its own without any conscious help from me.

At least I was used to flying solo and handling shit myself. Most of the time I preferred it. I could talk to Harry. He was one more confidant than I'd had as a kid.

Justin

Even though I preferred small gatherings and time to myself, I was behaving myself at Britt's party. Trying to be social, even though it was exhausting for someone like me who pegged the introvert scale. It wasn't that I didn't like people. I wasn't antisocial. It was that being around lots of them wore me out and sapped my energy.

I smiled and nodded at a blur of introductions on the terrace of Britt's apartment building. She lived a couple blocks from Kay's West Seattle apartment. I hadn't realized how much I'd upset her routines and social life. She had a large circle of friends. Did she miss being so near them?

When I'd proposed this crazy solution to my marital and business problems, I hadn't had time to think through everything. I worked all the time. I hadn't stopped to think Kay would be different. That she was probably as extroverted as I was introverted. That she would feed off the energy of being around others. That I was proposing a mixed marriage of sorts.

The terrace faced west, angled to get the optimum view of the jagged Olympic Mountains and the sun as it set over them. Britt and company had festooned the party space with crepe paper and flowers. Though Kayla enthused over the beautiful pink, saying it was just the color she would have chosen, to me everything was the dull gray of a rainy day.

Britt had style. Her party décor highlighted it. She'd already buzzed around me, hinting, broadly, about a senior merch job at Flash. Damn, I could have given her one on the spot, I supposed. But going over the head of the VP of merchandising would have pissed her off. All the power of the universe of my company. And yet restricted by social conventions and employee relationships.

I made a mental note to put in a good word for Britt. Subtly. So my VP thought hiring Britt was her idea. We poached talent from Britt's current employer, our bigger, badder rival across town, regularly. There was nothing out of the ordinary about snatching one of their people. I wasn't convinced, however, that having my wife's best friend working for me was the best idea. I wasn't sure I could avoid it, either. And live in any kind of marital bliss.

A wedding cake—covered in gray fondant that I was told was pink, white polka dots, gray/pink and white flowers trailing over the side—sat on a table, center stage. With yet another cake topper in the showcase position. *Let them eat cake* was becoming our motto.

It was an interesting study in human behavior to see how romantic or sentimental or comedic this group of Kay's friends was. I was surprised, though maybe I shouldn't have been, by their selection. It was clearly a joke. One that Kay seemed amused by this time.

A stoic, nerdy, skinny groom, cleanly shaved, again, held a flamboyant bride with a lush figure and beautiful breasts peeking out of a low-cut gown in his arms. She had one leg flung up in celebration, flashing leg and garter, pink flowers—I supposed they were pink, anyway—held to her hair. It was like she was saying, *Look what I caught!*

The cake topper bride was kissing her nerdy groom, lips puckered, neck extended as she reached to press her lips to his chaste, closed lips. His eyes were shut. He looked as devoid of emotion as the statue he was. Passionless as he let her kiss him.

Was this how they saw me? Vanilla? Without personality? And Kay throwing herself at me? Proud that she'd caught the billionaire?

I thought this wedding topper was more offensive than Lazer's, which had been blatantly jocular. But that was me. And I was presumably the butt of this one.

At some point, we were going to have to cut that gray cake. I wasn't looking forward to the scrutiny and all eyes on me. What would Britt, the emotional savant, see? What had she seen? A sexually frustrated guy with smoldering passion? With unrequited love shining in his eyes and a boner that wouldn't go away? A guy who was in love with a girl not just for her body, but for the whole package—her wit, her intelligence, her kindness?

If Britt were as emotionally smart as she claimed to be, she would see all of that and more. But I wasn't going to make it easy for her. Why should I? Why would I?

The view from the terrace was breathtaking, the Pacific Northwest at its finest. The sound sparkled, lit up by the sinking sun and silhouetting the mountains. The evening was warm and clear. From all outward appearance, Kayla seemed to be enjoying herself as she flashed her ring and her friends gushed over it. I was embarrassed by it. It should have been bigger. Showier. Damn it! Just more. The whole damn marriage should have been more.

As the booze flowed, the talk grew louder. I tried to be good-natured about the ribbing I got from almost everyone. High school. Childhood. College friends. I could see the wheels turning in all of them—why the hell had she chosen *him*? He's not *her* type at all. Money aside, of course. Hard to resist that kind of cash. Very recently a billionaire. Too recent to have developed much emotional maturity. Poor douche. He *must* have business sense. He can't be completely stupid. But emotionally? He's been had. She'll leave him. Sooner, if not later. No, sooner. Indecently soon, probably. And take as much of his fortune with her as she can. I just hope she leaves him a piece of his heart.

This could be one of those marriages measured in weeks. What has it been already? A week? Hmmm, that's pushing it.

Kay had complained to me, upset about being seen as a gold-digging woman. Worried her friends would see things that way. Concerned about the story we'd made up to explain our sudden passion.

I didn't blame her. But she hadn't thought through the other side of the equation. My side. That people saw me as an idiot. That when she left I'd be the fool.

A year gave me some credibility, some plausible deniability. She hadn't married me *just* for my money. There'd been something else. A spark. An ID thief. I laughed inwardly. I could deny being a fool. Things just hadn't worked out. Love fades and fails sometimes. That's just the way it is. She wanted to be the one who left me. Wanted me to be the bad guy so she could save her dignity.

Like hell. I was going to fight to keep her to the bitter end. She didn't know it yet, but she was going to have to be the villain. She was going to have to leave me. I wasn't going to make it easy for her. She'd have to walk out on me. And I would play that broken heart for all it was worth. In public. Anywhere I could. It wouldn't be hard. I'd simply have to let my true emotions show. The brokenhearted billionaire. I hoped I didn't have to be that guy.

Currently, I may have been the baby billionaire. But in the business world I was confident and commanded respect. I was as in control as the wild ride of the business world allowed. I felt insecure as hell among Kay's friends and blond sorority sisters from college. Kay had been in the most prestigious sorority at the university. The one with the hottest girls. And I'd been...a dweeb.

At the same time, I was tripping on the power of being a billionaire. It was still new to me. I hadn't grown into the role. But with the newness came excitement. Everything glowed. The novelty of a billionaire in their midst created a stir. People were reverent toward me now. Polite. Sycophantic. It amused me. And was disturbing, at the same time, that money could change every perception.

I recognized many of the guests. Kelly, the former house president. Morgan, who'd been the bitch of the sorority house, and her guy, frat boy Dakota. Alexis, who was a pledge when I met her. Zach, the houseboy who caused her fall from grace. Seth, another houseboy friend of Kay's. And Maddie. Kay had a habit of slumming with the underdogs. Like houseboys. And me. And treating them with kindness and respect. In other words, like regular people.

Our wedding reception with her friends was like a college class reunion. Kay was the princess. I vowed to treat her like one, too. Lazer may have made her an exaggerated video game character. But I could give her the royal treatment in real life. I could one up him and make her my queen.

I was the guy no one recognized. Time and again people told me the same thing: "I can't believe how much you've changed! I wouldn't have recognized you. Of course, I've seen your picture in the media in recent years. But it's hard to believe you're the *same* Justin we knew in college."

Their tone, their wonder, wasn't exactly flattering. But I think they *meant* to be complimentary.

Eventually, I excused myself to use the restroom. When I returned, I stood on the edge of the crowd, watching. I didn't belong in this world. For a second I wondered if Kay belonged in mine.

I wasn't good at one-on-one chitchat with strangers. At breaking into intimate, small groups. Kayla was in her element. Dressed in a lacy white sundress and looped with pearls, she looked every inch a bride as she floated through the crowd, chatting with her friends. Laughing. Enjoying herself. If I could have stopped time and held on to her forever, I would have.

She was stunning to look at. No one would ever believe me, but her looks weren't the main attraction for me. Yeah, sure, my body reacted to her. But it was her personality, her mind, that intrigued me and turned me on. She hid behind her looks, like I did behind mine. Mine made me invisible, made people discount me as a threat. Made me the butt of jokes. Kay's drew attention. Drew the eye. People assumed because she was pretty, she wasn't smart. We were more alike than she thought. If only she'd step back and take the time to see it.

Someone slapped a hand on my back. I jumped.

"Dude! You got it *bad.*" Dex, Kayla's cousin, and my buddy from college, had clapped a hand on my shoulder.

I'd been engrossed in my thoughts. I hadn't heard him approach.

He squeezed my shoulder. "If it isn't the blushing bridegroom."

"I never blush." I broke into a smile.

"You're full of shit. You're the blushingest guy I know."

I looked over my shoulder at him. "Finally! A friendly face. Where the hell have you been? You're late."

Dex laughed. "Traffic. I had to park half the city away." He studied me. "What are you doing lurking in the shadows? Shouldn't you be front and center?"

I shrugged. "Preserving my sanity. Grooms are just an accessory at wedding functions these days anyway. A necessary evil."

Dex comically cocked an eyebrow. He was a good four or five inches shorter than I was. In college, he'd been taller than me. He hadn't had the advantage of an unexpected late growth spurt. He was still the same, but better dressed than usual. Typically Dex dressed like most of the geek techies you saw around Seattle, in jeans and a T-shirt. Kayla's fashion sense, and owning Flash, must have been rubbing off on me. Before I wouldn't have noticed.

Dex studied me. "You look...nice. Lala's making you over already?" He laughed. "Never thought my cousin would marry a fixer-upper like you, dude. She's slumming it."

I grinned. Damn, it was good to see Dex. "Look at you, too, man. You look halfway styling. Your mom pick out your clothes?"

He grinned and squirmed. He was wearing a sport coat and jeans. "Shows what you know. Mom's an engineer, not a fashion plate. My nerdiness is genetic. If I look good, it's purely accidental." He winked.

Kayla spotted us and hurried over to hug her cousin, saving me from a response. "You're late!"

"Is there an echo in here?" Dex grinned at me. "Your better half just said the same thing. Traffic." He shrugged again.

"Better half, is he?" Kay slid her arm through mine and smiled that world-lighting smile at me, as if I made *her* dreams come true.

The smile was genuine enough. The magnitude of emotion behind it was faked. But damn, I'd take it anyway.

She squeezed my arm and put a tease in her voice. "He's been hiding out here on the periphery since I introduced him around."

"Smart choice," Dex said. "A guy can only take so much small talk. What do you expect? A pound of flesh?" He made a gun with his hand and pointed it to his head. "Pwhoooo."

"Dex!" She laughed at his antics. "You're horrible. Play nice. These are my friends."

Their mothers were twins, but they didn't look anything like cousins. Kay was slender and willowy, freaking gorgeous. And Dex was...well, Dex. Short, skinny, and geeky. He had a certain charm, though.

"Hey! I wouldn't even be here, but Mom made me. She was all, 'You have to support your cousin. You don't want to hurt her feelings, do you?'" He spoke in a high-pitched voice, mimicking his mom. "I told her you wouldn't even miss me. You'd be too busy with your crowd."

Kay shook her head. "Misguided fool! I certainly *would* have noticed the lack of grief I was getting. You're always such a soothing presence." She leaned toward him. "I'm glad Auntie made you come." She hitched a thumb at me. "You can keep this antisocial one company." She smiled up at me and stroked my beard before tipping her face up and kissing me. Her lips were soft and moist and gently parted for effect.

I called her bluff and pressed her to me, taking advantage of her open lips and darting my tongue in. She didn't expect a French kiss. Or the way I playfully tickled the roof of her mouth with my tongue, daring her to squirm or laugh when she was so obviously putting on a romantic show.

"Bastard!" she whispered in my ear, laughing, when she pulled away.

Dex was staring at us with narrow eyes, the picture of suspicion.

"Go!" I squeezed her ass, playfully. Because I could get away with it here. Because I wanted so much more. "Mingle with your friends. Dex and I will be outcasts together."

"Get him something to drink immediately, will you? Booze takes the edge off his sharp tongue." She blew us both a quick kiss.

I watched her float away, her lacy skirt blowing around her in the gentle breeze.

"Sharp tongue? I don't know what she's talking about. It's not just sharp. It's lethal." Dex grinned. "She's right, though. If I'm going to make it through the two hours I promised Mom I'd stay, I need a drink."

I escorted Dex to the bar, meaning table full of buckets filled with ice and alcohol, and waited while he grabbed a locally made beer and a plate of appetizers. We found an empty table on the outskirts of the crowd and sat, watching the sunset.

As soon as we were settled, he turned to me. "How the hell did you pull this one off?"

I stared at him. "Pull what off?"

I played innocent. But I knew full well what he meant. I'd been concerned about fooling Britt. Now Dex was hitting me with the surprise attack. He knew both of us too well and was too damned smart to be in the dark long. He didn't need emotional intelligence. He was logical and as observant as hell. Half the time I wondered if he'd already been recruited by the CIA. If not, they were missing out.

"The hell you don't. How did you get my hot cousin to marry *you*? What prank did you use to pull it off?"

I continued the innocent act. "What makes you think she *didn't* marry me for my lovable self?" I looked past him, toward the sunset.

"Or your piles of money?" He set his beer down. "Cut the shit. She's not in love with you. That's plain enough to see."

I swallowed hard. Dex never pulled his punches. He wasn't cruel. Just brutally honest in the bluntest way possible.

He was right. But hearing it from him still felt like a blow to the gut.

"I've seen her in love," he said before I could respond. "And this ain't it. I'm not trying to hurt your feelings, dude. Just honestly reporting what I see."

I turned my gaze on him.

"Don't give me those hurt puppy eyes, Green. Save them for you wife."

"Puppy eyes?" I snorted. "You're full of it."

He laughed. "Hey, I'm on *your* side here. I actually *like* you. That's a first. Trust me. Lala has terrible taste in men. Always has. Since elementary school when she had her first crush on the bully who was the school's best jock."

He leaned toward me. "You're not her type, Green. Not at all. You, the two of you, are very convincing tonight, though. I'll give you that much. You should think about trying out for community theater." He laughed. "It's too bad for you that I'm completely unfoolable. How *did* you pull it off?"

I stared at him. "You're full of shit."

He shook his head, clearly amused by my denial. "Cut the crap. Here's the deal. I'm an only child. Lala's an only. Our moms are twin sisters and thick as thieves. Especially given they're just fraternal twins. Enough said.

"I know my cousin. I've been subjected to her fantasies of her ideal man practically since birth. You aren't it, Green. Not even close. Not even with your billions. My cousin likes money. Don't we all? But she's too romantic, and lusts after athletic bodies too much, to sell out love and physical chemistry for dollars." He sighed, like that was a real weakness of hers.

True, I thought. But she *could* be convinced to help a friend in need out by taking a job as his wife. Provided there was an expiration date to the marriage.

"Don't get me wrong." When Dex was on a roll you couldn't shut him up with a 6.9 magnitude earthquake. He said so himself. He actually did talk through the one we had when we were little and in elementary school.

I didn't know him then. The quake bounced me right off the grass of the playground onto the dirt of the ball field and back. And was an exciting distraction from the pain of recess.

Dex was answering a question in class and calmly got beneath his desk as the building shook. He didn't stop talking and expounding on his answer, even though everyone else was screaming and crying for Mommy. He answered correctly, too. According to him. And got an A, naturally. And a lasting interest in seismic activity.

"She could do a whole hell of a lot worse than you." He pointed at me for emphasis, his eyes bright with excitement. Dex loved a good detective story. "I even told her that in college. I was putting in a good word for you, man, even then. You, at least, have a brain. And a heart, I think. If you'd get it out of your ass and actually use it to win her."

My death stare didn't stop Dex.

"You're not like that complete douche Eric. But she *was* in love with him. As recently as eight days ago." Again with the piercing stare. Dex would make a world-class interrogator. "Hung all over him as if she couldn't wait for him to touch her. Practically wiped his feet for him. It's a pity. And a joke. She has such good taste in everything else."

Dex sighed again, resigned to Kay's fault. "It's her sense of physical aesthetics that's throwing her off. If she could get past wanting that physical perfection fantasy, she'd have a shot at happiness." He continued to hold my gaze.

Dex was hypnotic that way. He knew how to arrest your attention.

"There's none of that fiery lust and romantic longing here for you." He tipped his head side to side in that way people do when they're weighing pros and cons and kind of going, eh! And toggled his hand side to side, fingers spread to indicate his indecision. "She likes you. That's something. A small start. But she's faking the rest. There's no lust for you."

He took another pull of beer and held it in his mouth for a second before swallowing. "Full-bodied." He read the label and raised a brow. "Smooth. Nice mouth feel. A good dark ale. I'll have to remember this one."

"Glad to hear you're on my side." I couldn't keep the sarcasm out of my voice. "With friends like you—"

"Who needs enemies?" he finished for me. "Original." He shook his head. "You can do better than that! Anyway, it's not like that at all. I just know a good piece of bullshit when I see it. And I'm seeing crap written all over this marriage."

He leaned even closer to me and lowered his voice to almost a whisper. "Eight days ago, you weren't even in her vocabulary. She was crying her eyes out over Eric. Then, suddenly, you're married and she's madly in love with you?" He held his hand out palm up, like, *Serious-ly? You expect me to believe that shit?*

"That's too farfetched even for a fairytale. Some-thing smells here. And it isn't these horrible crab puffs." He laughed. "Remember the guide for getting girls we invented in college? You followed it to the let-ter when you created Flash. Target rich environment. Making yourself indispensible. Putting yourself in a position of power. I'm proud of you, dude." He paused, his eyes twinkling. "So. What prank are you running?"

I stared at him, keeping my emotions masked. "There's no prank." I glanced across the room at Kay. My pulse roared at the sight of her, like it always did. I smiled involuntarily.

Dex shook his head. "Damn, you have it bad for her. Always did."

He paused to take another drink of beer. "Let's play the facts back. Kay went to Reno on business after Eric broke her heart. She returns home to her apartment. No mention of you. No mention of having met someone. No nothing on any of her social media accounts. She stays in, sick as a dog from food poisoning through Sunday. On Monday, a large black vehicle pulls up in front of her building and she's served with papers. A divorce summons. From you. The next day, your happy marriage is all over the news." He paused. Dex had a flair for the dramatic. "Tell me. How far off am I?"

"Nice story. Ever thought of writing a novel?" I took a sip of beer to calm down and put on my poker face. I was good at poker. Too bad this wasn't a card game. How the hell had Dex discovered all this? The sneaky little bastard.

He laughed. "Whatever prank you pulled, it's epic. Just don't hurt my cousin. Or I'll have to ruin you." Which sounded like your average idle threat. But Dex was dead serious. And he could probably do it if he wanted to. He already had a bunch of damning facts in his possession.

"Wouldn't dream of it." I tried to sound amused. "As you say, I'm in love with her."

"Isn't that sweet!" He eyed me cautiously. "That's not the end of my story, however."

"There's more?"

"I'm just getting to the interesting part. Suddenly, your digital fingerprint is all over the Internet. You're using our code. Face Find, the facial-recognition software we wrote together in college. The one we used to find the hot chicks we saw on campus and were too afraid to talk to." Again with the dramatic pause. "You're looking for something. More accurately, someone. Who is it? What's going on, Green? What have you gotten yourself into? Let me in on it, too. I can help."

I shrugged. His offer was tempting. "I'm always looking for something. Watching my competitors. There's nothing out of the ordinary in that."

He laughed. "I don't believe you." He glanced across the room to where Kay was talking with her friends and casting surreptitious glances our way when they thought we weren't looking.

What were they saying about me? Were they as suspicious as Dex?

"Look, if I can find this much out this easily, others can, too," Dex said, reasonably. "Whatever you're up to, watch yourself, man. And remember, me and my superior coding skills are here for you whenever you need my help."

"Good to know." My gaze lingered on Kay. That stupid smile was still on my face, the one I couldn't suppress.

Dex gave me a pitying look and shook his head. "I wouldn't do this for just anybody. But I'm going to help you out with my cousin—since you conned her into marriage somehow you have my grudging respect. And the moms—hers and mine—are going to be hellcats if this marriage breaks up. Family harmony means so much to me!" His eyes danced.

"I don't know much about love. But I'd suggest scouring the Internet and finding something doused in pheromones to induce at least a little lust. She's always fondly said you were sweet. You may be able to use that to your advantage. That's something new to her in a man.

"Your real advantage will be to treat her like she has a brain. She inherited the Harrington smarts from our moms. But people rarely get past her looks. And her interest in style and fashion. They don't see her creative side for the intelligence it is, and wrongly peg her as a superficial dumb blond. Appreciate that and she might fall for it. You have the perfect business for her. Use Flash to your advantage. Get her involved in it."

His eyes were sharp as he continued to stare at me. He sighed. "You can con a girl into a date. Into bed. And, shit, evidently into marriage. But how the hell do you prank them into falling in love with you? If you find out, dude, you have to share."

He sighed. "Let me give you another piece of advice about Lala. If you don't want to lose her, integrate her into your life in *every* way possible. Intricately weave her in. Get her involved in Flashionista. Hire her. Give her a job. She loves that fashion shit and she's good at it. Keep her busy.

"A little-known fact about Lala—she doesn't like change. Weave her in, make her comfortable in your life, and she'll have a hard time extracting herself from it. Crap, who would want to leave the billionaire life-style anyway, right?"

I shook my head, acting like he was talking crazy. "You're bizarre."

"And highly analytical. Like you. Have you already calculated your odds of success with her?" He laughed. "You must have, or you wouldn't have tried this stunt." He paused. "One last thing, the logical extension of all this—she likes kids. She's always wanted them. The way she used to cart around her baby doll—" He got an evil look in his eye.

I felt for that baby doll. I was pretty sure he'd used it to prank Kayla somehow.

"Get her pregnant," he said. "Give her a baby. She'll fall in love with her baby. And maybe, by extension, you. She won't easily want to leave her baby daddy. Especially not when he can give the kid every advantage."

I stared at him like he was crazy. And felt myself flush.

Dex's eyes went big and round. He swore beneath his breath. "Dude! You haven't *slept* with her? She's your *wife*. Exercise those marital rights." He shook his head in apparent disbelief. "This gets more and more interesting by the minute. Why should I be surprised? Something about this whole wedding business has been off since the beginning."

"You're really full of BS," I said.

"I wish I were. But I'm not. I've been studying micro expressions. You know how it is when I study something." He laughed. "I master it! Sexual frustration. Longing. Shock. Embarrassment. They all crossed your face in the space of a second. Micro expressions don't lie. They're involuntary."

"You're way off." He was right. Micro expressions didn't lie. "I'm not ready for kids. That's what you saw. We haven't even talked about them yet."

"Liar." He shook his head, laughing softly to himself. "You are so full of shit you're turning brown. I don't know how you tricked her into marrying you. Or what crazy deal you struck. I hope you aren't still using your old method of acting indifferent so the girls come to you. If that's your plan, you're screwed. Though not literally." He laughed again. He was thoroughly enjoying himself.

"Get over yourself and tell her how you feel. Often and with feeling. Girls eat that shit up. Tell her you want to sleep with her." He sighed, shaking his head. "I never thought I'd say this—bed my cousin. The sooner, the better. Take her home tonight and make love to her."

He downed the rest of his beer and looked around the party. "Lala has some hot friends. This isn't a wedding, but close enough. Girls will be in a romantic mood." He winked at me. "Grooms make the best wingmen. Come on, junior birdman." He nodded to me. "Help me separate one from the herd."

CHAPTER THREE

Kayla

"I never thought I'd say this," Britt said, "but there's something magnetic about Justin. He's not classically handsome. But he does have a nice body."

Her tone reminded me of the silly question we used to ask each other as girls—if you could only have one of these combinations in a guy, a great body and a hideously ugly face or a classically handsome face and a soft, squishy body, which would you choose?

"And he's...what's the word I'm looking for?" She frowned and looked around the group of my friends for help. Like this was a game of wedding Scrabble or something.

I shrugged and held my hands up, not particularly in the mood to help her denigrate my groom. Or was she complimenting him? It was hard to tell.

"It doesn't matter. I'll think of it later. He *definitely* turns heads." The surprise in her voice was a bit unsettling. She bit her lip, studying him while he sat at a table talking with Dex.

I was happy Jus and Dex were occupied with each other. It kept them out of trouble. Dex was animatedly expounding on some point or other, gesturing for emphasis like he did when he was excited. Probably regaling Jus with some latest theory on coding or something technical that would have bored everyone else here.

"That beard," Britt said with an unnerving awe in her voice. "That lovely, luscious beard. I think it's the beard. It's hot. Just looking at it makes me want to run my fingers through it. Though God knows, there could be a hideous, weak chin beneath it."

"Are you crazy?" I gave her my "you're insane" look. I realized my mistake too late. "No weak chin, by the way. And keep your hands off my husband's face."

She laughed. "I'm disappointed in you, Kayla. Beards are *totally* in style now. The absolute latest, hottest trend. *You* should know that, Mrs. Flashionista. Justin gets points on this one for being more up on men's grooming trends than you are."

Even my best friend couldn't get away with insulting my sense of style. "Jus? Stylish?" I made a sound of disbelief. "You should have seen that thing before I got hold of it."

Morgan and Alexis were standing with us. Their gazes had turned to Jus. They wore that critical look women have when they're evaluating men, particularly other girls' guys.

"She's right." Morgan nodded. "That *is* a particularly nice, healthy, and soft-looking specimen of male virility." She winked at me.

I tried not to roll my eyes. That would only encourage them.

"He's almost hipster. Very Seattle." Morgan took a deep breath. "He's certainly grown into his looks. He used to be all sharp angles and bones. Awkward. Now he looks like he's totally hard planes and muscle." She paused. "I wish I could get Dak to grow a nice, full beard. But his style is frat-boy preppie and, now, clean-shaven corporate."

I looked to Alexis for help.

"Sorry!" She flashed an apologetic grin. "I agree with the girls. Seattle girls like beards. And I'm a Seattle girl through and through. Zach never gets farther than a few days' growth before he shaves. I'm going to convince him a beard is the way to go." She winked at Morgan.

"When I heard about your marriage, I was as shocked as anyone." Morgan swirled her glass of champagne. "But look at the way he looks at you!"

They all turned to stare at him. He glanced at us and looked quickly away, like we'd caught him looking and scared him off.

"He's head over heels. That, in itself, is priceless. Eric always treated you with such indifference. As if he could take you or leave you. As if he expected you to adore him and it was his right to take you for granted." Morgan wiped the condensation from the bottom of her glass with a napkin she held.

Morgan was a recovering alcoholic. She was drinking sparkling cider. So I couldn't even claim she was impaired.

"*I* wouldn't have set you two up. But I would have been wrong. I'm big enough to admit it. Now you can invite me to your fiftieth, where I'll toast your good sense for ignoring what the rest of us used to think." Morgan laughed.

We all laughed. Me nervously. Fifty years of marriage? Twice our current lifetimes yoked to the same person? It seemed unimaginable. But she had *no* idea.

"I approve, too," Alexis said. "Not that you need *my* approval. But I think you've found something special."

She nodded ever so slightly in Justin's direction. "Look at the way he looks at you when he thinks you're not looking. He's a man who's desperately in love. I hope you'll forgive me for the times I made fun of him in college. He was such a sweet, awkward, young thing." She laughed. "He's really grown into a striking guy."

"Striking! That's it. That's the word I was looking for." Britt smiled, smug in the confirmation of her thinking. "Or maybe arresting. Something about him draws the eye."

Lord have mercy! As my grandma used to say. I downed my entire glass of champagne and poured myself another. My friends loved Jus. I felt like I'd gone through the looking glass into an alternate world.

"I think it's time to cut the cake." Britt took my arm and shepherded me toward it, waving at Jus to join us.

Jus and I had the patter, our routine, of cutting the cake down like two comedians who played the same gig night after night.

When we finished, Britt handed us a bottle of champagne. Jus popped the cork, neatly avoiding my dress with the spray as Britt and the girls served the guests.

Dex stepped forward to make the first toast to us, the ostensibly happy couple.

"Justin didn't have a best man. As the sole representative of his friends, and also as a relative of the bride, it's my duty to stand in and make a toast." He cleared his throat and raised his glass. "Green, you got the best girl in the family. No matter that she's the *only* girl. Take good care of her. Or else. You *know* I can out-prank you."

The crowd laughed. There was a catch in Dex's voice that made me teary. He usually teased me mercilessly. But here he was, being sweet and emotional.

Even though I knew this marriage was a lie, a convenience, a job, even, in the comfort of my friends, it was easy to forget all that. To feel what they felt—happiness for Jus and me. Happiness and belief in new and surprising love. Joy. There was so much bad crap in the world all the time. It was fun to celebrate something. Like us.

I was immensely pleased that my friends, who I'd feared wouldn't approve of my marriage to Justin or would lecture and tease me about marrying him for his money, were one hundred percent supportive. They loved him, were awed by him, were swept away by this illusion of love and happiness we'd pulled off. They, the people who knew me best, could see me being swept off my feet by *him*. Not his money. *Him.* Not one person implied otherwise. They were as surprised as I was. I loved them all for it more than I could say.

I should have felt guilty about fooling my best friends in the world. I *did* feel guilty. To a degree. But all the champagne I'd had had gone to my head. And made me feel floaty and flirty, like alcohol always did. Elated.

"Kayla."

At the sound of my name on Dex's lips, I startled out of my thoughts. He was staring directly at me with that sappy, almost brotherly, teasing look on his face.

"Justin is one of my good friends. Treat him with love and respect. And please, take the familial pressure off me, and make many beautiful, brainy babies with him to keep our moms happy and off my back about grandchildren! To Justin and Kayla and many, *many* happy years together!"

As glasses clinked around us, I smiled up at Jus. He pulled me into his arms and kissed me. Everyone expected it. And maybe it was the bubbles or the buzz of the alcohol, but I felt a spark. A tiny spark of *something* as his beard brushed my lips. I almost didn't want the illusion to end.

It was just a week off the summer solstice. Nearly the shortest night of the year. By the time the party ended, dawn was just a few short hours away. I offered to help Britt clean up, but she shooed me away.

"I can handle this. Go make some beautiful babies with that brainiac of yours!" She winked and laughed. And handed me a white paper bag with twine handles filled with leftover appetizers, a large piece of wedding reception cake, and the cake topper.

There was enough innuendo in her tone to let me know what she meant. Her advice hadn't changed since Thursday: *Get pregnant now.* I wished we hadn't run into Lazer at lunch. I wished she hadn't seen me flirt with him. If she hadn't caught the way I'd looked at Lazer, she would have completely believed my charade with Jus.

The evening had been too good to let anything spoil it, even Britt's outrageous advice. I was high on success. Light. Buzzed to almost drunk on champagne.

I hung on Justin's arm, gazing at him adoringly in case any of my friends were still in sight.

Outside, Jus pulled the keys from his pocket. They nearly fell through his fingers. He lunged and caught them. We broke out laughing, though it wasn't that funny.

"I hope no cops saw that!" I smiled into his eyes. "Think you could pass a sobriety test?"

"We should have thought ahead and taken the service. I didn't think there would be so much booze at this thing." He whipped out his phone. "I'll call the car service."

"No!" The night was too good to be ruined waiting for a car. "My apartment is just a few blocks away.

Let's spend the night there. We can walk to our little love nest." Had I just said "love nest"? I was being way too flirty.

"Too bad Carl, my building manager, doesn't work on Sundays. It would help our cause if he saw us together." I looked up at Jus with bedroom eyes. I wasn't sure what I was promising.

But he swallowed hard and took the white bag from me. "I'll text Magda and ask her to look in on Data first thing in the morning."

I nodded and waited for him to send his text. "Isn't the night beautiful!" I couldn't contain my happiness and relief as we walked hand in hand, staggering slightly, and tripping on cracks and dips in the rough concrete sidewalks.

I let us into my apartment and collapsed onto the sofa, kicking my shoes off and sighing with pleasure. "We did it! The evening was a roaring success. I was *so* nervous about it. My friends know me better than anyone, even my mom.

"I hadn't realized how worried I was that they would think badly of me, like everyone else, and accuse me of marrying you just for your money. Which is true. In a way. But they loved you!"

Jus set the white bag on my miniscule kitchen counter. It was just plain laminate. My apartment had very little gingerbread, as Dad called it. But it was nice. Jus stripped off his jacket, tossed it over a barstool at the kitchen counter, plopped onto the sofa next to me, and kicked off his shoes, too.

I tucked my legs beneath me. "They loved us! Better, everyone believed in us. We even won Britt over. You charmed them." I sighed, trying not to sound as surprised as I felt. "Even Dex behaved himself—"

I frowned at Justin. "You're being very quiet. What's wrong?" I stroked his arm. "I'm talking too much. I'm sending you confusing signals. When you captivated my family, I was upset. Now I'm ecstatic. Which will it be, girl?" I laughed. "I know! I'm terrible. Women can be so confusing!"

"This time, though, you weren't trying to impress them. You were just being you. I can't fault you for that."

A quick look of something—happiness or eagerness or maybe hopefulness—crossed his face. He was quiet a moment.

When I didn't keep rambling on, his expression clouded. "Dex suspects." Jus sprawled and leaned his head back against the sofa cushion.

"What?" I couldn't have heard right. "Suspects what?"

"That our marriage isn't real."

"Dex? Dex of *all* people? He gave that beautiful toast—"

"That was just bullshit. Dex giving me a bad time and yanking my chain." He sighed. "It's my fault." Jus stared at the ceiling. "My virginity gave us away."

"A virgin!" I couldn't help laughing, delighted with the admission and the ludicrousness of it. "But you were a married man before I took this job as your wife.

That stupid ID thief showing up with a baby she claims is yours is one of my darkest fears."

He slid me a sideways look. "Mine, too."

He hesitated. "I don't think I had sex with her." He shook his head. "The evidence is against it. If we did, I don't remember it. So I'm the same as." His Adam's apple bobbed. "As far as I know, I *am* a virgin. That's what Dex saw." He sighed again, heavily, embarrassed. "With my vast seduction skills, was there ever any doubt I was?"

I realized a second too late I should have kept my mouth shut. How would I know he was a virgin unless someone had told me? He was probably wondering who. And that computer-sharp mind of his had probably already figured out the culprit. "That's crazy."

"That I'm a virgin?" He looked confused and almost, but not quite, pleased that I believed he looked strictly non-virginal. "It's purely accidental."

I stroked his arm, which was delightfully hard and muscled, to soothe his vanity and reassure him it didn't matter to me. "No, I meant about *looking* like a virgin? I mean, maybe a girl's vagina can look that way during a doctor's exam. But how, exactly, does a guy look like a virgin?"

He closed his eyes and took a deep breath, shaking his head. "You'll have to ask your cousin for the specifics. He claims my virginity is like a blinking beacon giving us away. Told me he could see it in my micro expressions."

I rubbed my feet. I'd been in heels too long. I rolled my eyes. "Dex and his stupid micro expressions. I for-

got all about them. I thought they were one of his pass-
ing phases." I bit my lip.

Jus sat up and gave me a completely earnest expression. "There's only one solution, you know. We have to
have sex. For the good of our deception. I'd do anything to save Flash. Even, and including, giving up my
virginity for the cause."

My mouth fell open. And then, maybe it was the alcohol—even the cool night air had done little to sober
me—but I started to laugh. "That is the most absurd,
ridiculous pick-up line I have *ever* heard."

"At least it's original."

I expected him to look wounded, like I'd just
stabbed his male ego with the end of a very sharp nail.
But he was grinning, roguishly, beneath that sexy-
smelling beard that everyone but me seemed to like.

"Look." He took my hands in his. "Kayla Lucas
Green, I would bear the hardship gladly. I *want* to sleep
with you. In the worst possible way. I'd have to be a
eunuch not to."

"You would?"

He nodded. "Why do you think I go to bed so late
and get up so early?" He took a deep breath. "Because I
sleep with a hard-on that lasts so long I think I may
need medical treatment to get rid of it."

I couldn't help myself: I laughed at the way he poked
fun at himself. "Oh, don't, please. Not on my account.
As they say, a hard man is good to find."

His eyes lit up. He rubbed my thumb with his in a
seductive, intimate way. "I kick myself every day for
agreeing to the no-sex requirement."

"Really?"

He nodded so solemnly, I laughed again.

"After the first night together, I was hoping I could seduce you. But then I remembered I'm no heartthrob or player. And then I tell myself, there's nothing in writing. What we have is a verbal agreement. A gentleman's agreement. And my thoughts are not a gentleman's at all."

I looked at him, shocked. And flattered. And confused. *So that's why he doesn't sleep with me. I never thought...*

"So you're saying it would be my word against yours, as far as the verbal contract goes," I said, leading him on and teasing him. "That what we have is a he-said-she-said thing. And that most courts, of course, are going to rule that some sex is expected in a 'marriage.'" I put a flippant tone in my voice, flirting with him despite my serious words.

"Consensual sex, I think, is the key in any marriage. Rape is still rape. I'd never force myself on you. I wouldn't know how."

I smiled again at his pathetic come-on. But I believed him that he wouldn't force me.

He sighed like all the weight of the world sat on his chest. "I'm a twenty-one-year-old, frustrated virgin who's having a hell of a time keeping his hands to himself, Kay. I was hoping you'd take pity on me. You could fulfill an adolescent fantasy of mine."

"What fantasy?" I said, cautiously.

"The one where a beautiful, blond, older woman shows me the ways of love and seduction." His eyes sparkled.

He was so incredibly adorable. And he smelled seductively of that beard oil that I was sure was laced with pheromones or something. And the alcohol and the illusion and pleasure of the party were affecting my senses. I tingled at the thought. Actually tightened deep inside. It had been so long since I'd had sex. And even longer since it had been good.

"Does my inexperience scare you?" he asked when I didn't respond. "Because it scares the hell out of me. I'm in this sexually frustrated position now. Of my own making. Obviously, I can take matters into my own hand. But that's not what I want. I'm a married man. Who's always in the public eye. With a public fantasy romance to maintain. I could cheat. As long as I'm discreet. But if I'm caught—"

At the mention of cheating, I felt the rage of unreasonable jealousy flair. I pictured him with Ophie, poised over her. Maybe she was a virgin, too. I wouldn't be surprised. I imagined the two of them finding their way together. Walking in on them and the superior smile she would give me. *He's mine now. I'm the one who took his virginity. You tossed him away.* That's what the look in her eyes would say to me.

"I have plenty of money to pay someone," he said. "But a prostitute or call girl? That's courting trouble. They have a tendency to rat out their clients. And they're not my thing."

He sighed again, comically. "I didn't think this marriage through thoroughly, as I think we mentioned before."

I put a finger to his lips. "Shhhhh. If you're going to seduce a woman, you have to know when to stop talking."

He went perfectly still. His eyes were round and dark. His breathing shallow and excited. When was the last time any guy had looked at me with such lust and awe? He didn't know how erotic it was.

"I've never had a virgin before." I pursed my lips, making an exaggerated point of thinking his suggestion over. "Or a billionaire. Or a bearded lover."

"Well, there you have it. Three in one. A perfect trifecta." His voice was husky. "You might not get that combination again in one package."

I nodded, trying to look serious. "Yes, exactly. It's particularly rare in men of my age. Both the billionaire thing and the virgin. Not so much the beard. Which, by the way, and I don't know why I'm telling you this, my friends all think is hot. So I would score some points there, too. Though I get those whether I actually do you or not."

I tapped my fingers together. "Tempting. Very tempting. Though I'm not sure I'm really the deflowering kind, something about the idea *is* exciting." I slid into his lap and straddled him, one knee on either side of him as I took his face in my hands.

His eyes grew darker by the minute. "In some cultures, people pay good money to take a person's virginity. I'm offering mine up."

I tipped his face toward mine. "I've never heard of anyone paying for a guy's virginity before."

"And here I thought about auctioning mine off. Bad business plan?"

"Shut up." I leaned down and pressed my lips to his.

He grabbed my hips and settled me against the bulge in his pants. He was right. He had a boner that wouldn't quit. For one quick sec, I flashed back to college and the way eager frat guys would press up against us sorority girls at their parties. Maybe it was Justin's youthful eagerness or his lack of experience that made the comparison in my mind.

The skirt of my dress billowed around us. My panties rubbed against his pants. I went wet. My body, obviously, had also been seduced by the party. The phrase *Fake it till you make it* took on a whole new meaning.

I broke away from Justin's sweet, desperate kiss, slid off his lap, stood, and took him by the hand. "Come with me and let me make a man out of you." I pulled him to the bedroom.

My apartment was small. No more than eight hundred square feet—entryway that was really just a pad, tiny kitchen, living room, bathroom, one bedroom. My bed was made, covered in a white, fluffy, lacy comforter set I'd gotten for a steal off Flashionista. My sheets were, fortunately, clean. Which, for some weird matter of pride, was important to me. New man and all.

Jus hesitated in the doorway. "Why do I feel like I should carry you over the threshold?"

I smiled at him. "Then do it."

He caught me beneath the knees and swept me into his arms. I threw my arms around his neck, kicked one leg high like our latest cake topper, and smiled at him.

"If this had been our real wedding night, I would have had flowers waiting." His voice was husky and surprisingly genuine.

I resisted asking if he'd done that on his real wedding night to the imposter. He didn't remember anyway, so the point was moot.

"Red rose petals covering the bed."

"Rose petals are messy and overrated." I stroked his bearded cheek.

"Champagne chilling."

"We've had enough of that already." Which was why we were on our way to the bed. I pushed the thought and good sense aside. My body—and surprisingly, even a little bit of my heart—wanted this. How many times did you get a chance to initiate a good friend into the world of sex and passion?

He swallowed hard and carried me into the room, closing the door with his foot surprisingly suavely.

"You're cute," I said. "There's no need to close the door. It's just us here."

"Just trying to provide another sound barrier between us and the neighbors."

"I see," I whispered. "So you're expecting noisy sex? Will you be disappointed if I'm not a screamer?"

"As long as you do this with me, I won't be disappointed by anything you do or don't do."

"Big words. Big talk." I ran my fingers through his hair and unbuttoned his shirt as he carried me into the room. "That door butts up against the hall."

"Every little bit of sound barrier helps."

"Shy?"

"Maybe." He swallowed hard.

I tried to remember how I felt my first time. Scared. Determined. Eager. The sex didn't live up to the promise of all the hype. It was better for guys. I hoped it was, at least. I wanted this first time for him to be something special.

"The walls of this building are concrete and very soundproof." I kissed his neck.

"Good." He took two strides to my full-size bed and stopped.

I watched his face as he assessed the situation—just how did he suavely open the bed and get rid of all those decorative pillows I had piled on top? Yes, I was something of a pillow freak. What was his engineer's mind thinking?

Eric would have set me down. We would have each grabbed an armful of pillows and tossed them into the corner. Then one of us would have thrown the covers back. We'd become a bit settled and clinical that way. But then we would have gone after each other like animals.

Jus set me on my back on the bed, tenderly. Falling onto me. Bracing over me. Staring at me as if I was the most gorgeous girl in the world and he was the luckiest guy. With one smooth motion, he swept the pillows off the bed. He slid his arm beneath me, around my waist, and kissed me with surprising expertise. His lips were warm. His tongue probed with just the right amount of insistence. And he tasted good.

At the same time, he slid his free hand up my thigh beneath my skirt, stroking his way up my bare leg. His hands were hot and strong. And even though he was the virgin, it felt like he was the one teasing me as he hooked a finger in my thong panties and slid them down.

I could have teased him and made him work to take them off. But he was a novice, after all. And I was surprisingly hot for him. I bent my leg and let him slide the panties off, then kicked them away to join the pillows on the floor.

"Very smooth," I whispered as I removed his shirt and circled his nipple with the tips of my fingernails until he shuddered.

His hand was still on my thigh. He slid it up to cup my butt and then his fingers slid between my legs, massaging and stroking me with gentle attention until I bloomed for him. His face was a study of concentration, like all he wanted to do was please me. But he was holding back and determined not to break while I took my time.

I moaned softly.

He mumbled something.

"Don't worry," I whispered back. "I'm waiting for you. But we still have way too many clothes on." I reached for his zipper.

"To hell with this." He stood and slid off his pants, briefs, and socks. He almost toppled over once, as he tried to remove his last sock, bouncing on one foot. He was completely adorable in his embarrassment. "Not so suave."

He didn't know that sex wasn't scripted and choreographed like in the movies. Accidents happened. Clothes didn't just fly off miraculously. And afterward, sex was messy.

"Oh, I don't know. The view's pretty good from here."

Silhouetted in the streetlight that filtered in through my bedroom curtains, he was hard and erect. Amply endowed.

I sat up and presented my back to him. "Unzip me."

His fingers fumbled. The zipper stuck at the point where the bodice met the skirt of the dress. He struggled with it. I could feel his embarrassment and impatience.

"Don't worry. Zippers always stick at the top of the skirt where the fabric's thickest," I whispered. "Just give it a good tug."

A second later, he succeeded and the dress fell away. I slid out of it and rolled over on my back, bracing on my elbows.

My eyes had adjusted to the dark. I could see the look of amazement and awe on his face.

His gaze drifted to my breasts. His face twisted in consternation. "Damn. What are those?"

I laughed. "Don't like my chicken cutlets?"

"What?"

"My press-on bra. We called them chicken cutlets in college."

He frowned like he was figuring out a puzzle. "As a virgin, I thought I was doing pretty well. Until now."

"Oh, you were." I grinned at him to reassure him and crooked my finger at him.

"Women like to have their nipples sucked. And guys like to suck them, so I hear." He slid onto the bed next to me and gingerly pointed to the cutlets. "Those have to go."

"Yes?" I raised an eyebrow. "So what are you waiting for?"

"I'm not exactly sure how to remove them. Is there glue or tape involved? What are they held on with?

"Suction." I took my breast in my hand and fondled it.

Justin's mouth fell open. His gaze was riveted on my breast and the hand I caressed it with.

When his breathing grew excited enough, I slid my finger beneath the silicone to break the seal, and pulled the cutlet off. My nipple popped out erect and ready for action. Justin's breath caught.

Here was where things always got sticky in the undressing action. Literally. This was my favorite, and newest, pair of expensive cutlets. Cutlets are, well, sticky, and pick up lint. Which ruins them. I didn't have their case handy. So I reached up and stuck the cutlet on the decorative mirror over my nightstand.

"See how easy that is?" I took his hand and put in on my breast. "Now you try."

If I thought I was the one teasing him, I was sadly mistaken. When his finger slid between the cutlet and my skin, my nipple went so tight and hot I almost climaxed. He stuck that cutlet to the mirror next to its mate and caressed my breast with reverence and awe. When he took it in his mouth, I almost melted right there. He sucked and circled my nipple with his tongue until I moaned softly. Which should have been his cue to slip inside me. But either his virginity was making him miss the signal, or he was having too much fun and was really, *really* a breast man.

"Jus," I finally had to whisper. "If you keep sucking like that, I'm going to climax without you."

He grinned the grin of the enormously pleased. And fortunately, he was still enormous, long, and hard.

I pulled him on top of me. An experienced guy would have dived right in. Jus hovered over me with that sweet, hesitant innocence.

"This part is easy." I hooked my legs around him and positioned myself beneath him, with the tip of his dick at my opening. "Go ahead and thrust."

He made the attempt. And missed. The horrified look on his face was so sweetly naïve. I grabbed him and positioned him properly, arching up to meet until his tip slid in.

"Thrust," I whispered again as I wrapped my legs around his back. "Thrust. Thrust. *Thrust*." I was like an oarsman counting strokes and keeping the rhythm. "Deeper!" I threw my head back.

With each thrust, he grunted.

"Deeper," I cooed. His slow, steady, controlled pace was driving me to the edge. "Deeper. That's it. A few more thrusts. All the way in." I squeezed him to me with my legs, digging my heels into his rock-hard back. Pulling the hard length of him into me.

He grunted and moaned until the full length of him was inside.

"Now rock." I rocked my hips against him. "Harder. You can go harder. I won't break." I gasped.

Our rhythm wasn't exactly perfect. But it wasn't awkward in that way it can be with a new lover.

"This is the most natural thing in the world, Jus." I cupped his head and stroked his hair. "Don't overthink it. Let yourself go."

"Are you ready?" he whispered into my neck. "I want you to be ready."

"Oh, sweetie, I'm ready."

"Thank God. I can't hang on any longer." He rocked into me and finally let go, losing himself in the rutting rhythm of sex. Raw, primal sex.

Again. And again. I arched against him and gasped as the waves of a climax crashed over me. Exquisite waves of pleasure that curled my toes and took my breath away. A virgin had given me the climax of my life.

He called out my name and grunted.

When it was over, he stared at me in wonder. A sheen of sweat covered us both.

"That was..." He rested over me, taking the weight off me, still inside. "There are no words. Do I have to come out?"

"I'm in no hurry." I smiled up at him. "Eventually, you'll slide out, whether you want to or not."

"I know that much." His grin deepened.

"So? How does it feel to have lost your virginity?" I stroked his beard. "I'm so proud of myself. I've made a real man out of you." I laughed softly.

"How soon can we do it again?" He nuzzled my neck.

"I guess that answers my question." I sighed dramatically. "I've created a monster."

"Well?" He was staring at me with the most eager expression I'd ever seen.

I sighed. But to my surprise, I wanted it again probably as much as he did. "As soon as you're hard again."

His face lit up. "That won't take long."

CHAPTER FOUR

Kayla

Traditionally, when you bring a piece of wedding cake home from the reception, you're supposed to put it beneath your pillow. Then you'll dream about your future groom. So the wives' tale goes. I suppose that doesn't work when you're the bride. Or, at least, it's not politically correct to be dreaming about your second husband on your wedding night to the first. But what about when you're just pretending to be the bride? And the cake wasn't beneath your pillow, but on the counter in the kitchen?

After another three rounds of sex, I fell asleep in Justin's arms before he could suggest a fourth. Without getting up to put a piece of cake beneath my pillow. I was sure that wasn't what Britt intended it for anyway. But it was pointless to put it in the freezer to eat on our first anniversary. Yeah, eating your wedding cake at your divorce was just too sarcastic.

I slept more soundly than I had in years. And dreamed of Justin. But he was old, with a long gray beard like Rip Van Winkle. Or Father Time. And, really, in the way dreams can be, he didn't look like Justin. But I knew it was him. There was a cake with golden flowers. And all of our friends, who looked old, too. My mind's eye had aged them all so that they were recognizable.

When I woke, Justin's young, strong arm was tucked around me protectively, possessively. In that first moment of wakefulness, I thought it was just a relic from the dream. The weight of it had to be that of my own arm. Yes, that had to be it.

Startled, I stopped just short of throwing it off me and screaming. I even hoped, for a minute, that it was my own arm that had fallen asleep. Ever done that? Woken up with your hand asleep on yourself, screamed, and picked it up to toss off and run away, then realize it was part of yourself?

But no, it was his. I was disoriented, still partly in that dream and what was supposed to have been our fiftieth wedding anniversary. Damn that Morgan for implanting that thought in me. I was disoriented. It took me a sec to realize we were in my room. In my bed.

The sun shone brightly, creeping through the curtains. And my head pounded. Too much champagne. I felt Justin's rhythmic breathing against my neck, and thought, *What have I done?*

Deflowering a virgin—is it deflowering when you take a guy's virginity? Why wasn't there an equivalent word? Someone should put that on one of those IQ tests to get into Mensa. You know, like what is the opposite of hibernation? On the surface, you would think it is to be awake, of course. You have to be smart enough to know it was estivation, to sleep during the high heat of summer rather than the cold of winter.

Anyway, I suddenly understood what guys find so exciting about virgins. Initiating them into the world of sex was exciting. So why did *I* feel sore like a virgin? Like I'd been the one who'd been touched for the first time? Who knew Jus would have so much enthusiasm for the act?

Then again, he may have been naïve and inexperienced, but he *was* a guy. So I probably should have expected as much.

And why did I get a sappy look on my face when I thought about last night? And feel a little trill in my heart? Who knew that a man so attentive and eager to please could be such a turn-on? And make an experienced lover like Eric look like a hack in the sack?

Crap. This was exactly what I was afraid of from the very first—the implications of the morning after. When I couldn't walk away. For a whole year. And I'd even been dumb enough to do it at my place.

While I lay there waking, I tried to analyze how I felt. I didn't regret having sex with my husband. It had been an experience I'd never forget. I even felt a tiny bubble of happiness. The sex had been fantastic. Jus was a quick learner, even in bed. Chalk one up for intelligent guys. I just hoped he didn't expect too much because of this. Read too much. Because, while I was developing a real affection for him, I still wasn't willing to commit to anything like a real for-life kind of marriage. Not saying he wanted one, either.

Maybe I was worrying over nothing. Maybe he saw it for what it was—a decoy-wife-with-benefits situation. Kind of like a friend with benefits, but a bit more committed. Obviously.

My head pounded. As gently as I could, I slid out from beneath his arm, pulled a robe on, and slipped out to the kitchen. I needed my proven hangover cure breakfast—coconut water to rebalance the electrolytes, and burnt toast. Yum, right? Back in college, Seth and Zach, my favorite houseboys and good friends, used to burn my toast for me on Sunday mornings.

And two pain relievers to knock back the headache. I had the pain relievers. And a couple of bottles of coconut water I'd left in the fridge. But I was fresh out of bread. I'd tossed it all out when I'd moved in with Jus. I didn't even have any in the freezer. I'd been too efficient cleaning things out. Crap.

I was standing at the counter, wondering if a burnt toaster pastry would do the trick. According to my nursing school friend in college, it was the burnt char that actually absorbed the alcohol and did the trick. Like the activated charcoal they gave poisoning victims at the emergency room. I wasn't sure, though, that I could stomach burnt toaster pastry. There was something so much more innocuous about burnt toast.

And besides, all I had was frosted strawberry flavor. I knew you could burn them. I'd accidentally done it before. But I'd never eaten one afterward.

I grabbed a kitchen towel, ready to fan the smoke away from the smoke alarm. And was staring at the toaster, turning the dial up full, with a foil toaster pastry packet in my hand when—

"Morning, beautiful."

I jumped like I'd been caught with another lover.

Jus lounged in the entrance to the kitchen in his boxers, his face fresh and dewy from sleep. His hair rumpled. And his shirt off. His arm up, perched against the wall to show off his bulging bicep. "You look guilty. What did I catch you in the middle of?"

His question was innocuous. The expression on his face was *not*. He looked like the bluebird of happiness had landed on his shoulder. Sly and knowing, as if the whole world could see he was now initiated into the world of the sexually active. And everyone should congratulate him now that he was part of the club. Way too expectant and joyous.

"You caught me red-handed about to charbroil a toaster pastry until it smokes." I sighed. "I suppose the smell would have woken you, if not the fire alarm going off." I waved the towel at him. "Which is why I'm armed with this."

He frowned, puzzled. "Why?"

I shrugged. "To swoosh the smoke away from the fire alarm so it doesn't go off."

"Let me clarify—what did that toaster pastry ever do to you? If you're worried I'm going to suddenly insist you start cooking, you can relax. Magda's job is safe."

I laughed and explained about hangover cures and how I had nothing for breakfast in the apartment. Except for the toaster pastry.

"And yet you want to immolate the one edible thing you have?" He looked and sounded so totally adorable.

I really was losing my head and common sense. I grabbed the last bottle of coconut water and handed it to him. "This will help."

"Who says I have a hangover?"

His eyes *did* look bright, and he seemed entirely too perky. And happy. Bright. Radiant. *Intimate.*

Crap. My body was responding to the way he looked at me. I was intimately tight and clenching. My breasts were budding. I pulled my robe up tight around my neck, suddenly acting like a nun or something. "Jus, about last night...we need to talk."

It didn't take Dex's expertise with micro expressions to read Justin's face. If you want to send a guy into a panic and induce buzz kill, utter the words *we need to talk.* He regained control quickly. But not before disappointment and hurt flashed across his face. His jaw set.

And then I thought, *Crap. I can't do this to him. I can't hurt him. And I don't want to.* I wanted him again.

My kitchen was so small it only took two steps to reach him. I put my arms around his neck and smiled up at him. "You can't go around making me so sore that *I* walk like a virgin every morning." I cupped his face. "You were good last night, Jus. Especially for a virgin."

His eyes lit up and his face became radiant. "You wouldn't be interested in another round?"

I raised an eyebrow. "You're incorrigible! And you need to work on your pick-up line. I believe I mentioned being sore."

His gaze held mine, intent and full of desire. "Sorry. I don't read social cues well." His grin let me know he was joking.

He read them well enough.

"You know how you can cure a hangover by having another glass of alcohol in the morning? I've heard it's similar with sex. If you're sore, you need to do it again. And again. You'll feel better."

"Firstly, that is *so* a myth about curing a hangover with more alcohol. And second, you're full of it. But you're cute when you beg." I grabbed his hand and seized my opportunity to make myself clear while he was in the vulnerable, panting-for-sex position and thinking with his dick. "But we only have fifty-one weeks left together. We may as well make the most of them."

I pulled him toward the bedroom. And as I'd guessed, he didn't resist.

After, when we were lying next to each other, trying to catch our breath, he grinned at me again. "Sex is messy. They never show that in the movies."

I laughed. "I know. No one ever reaches for the towel." I grinned at him. "You've obviously never seen that chart about how many calories you use during sex, broken down by activity. Reaching for the towel, ten calories." I took a deep breath. "I'm famished."

"Do people really say famished anymore?" he teased.

"I just did."

He rubbed my arm. "Let me take you out for breakfast."

"Great idea!" I sat up. "Let me take a quick shower first."

He sat up, too, with that glint in his eyes.

I shook my head. "Alone. Shower sex is an advanced technique. We'll save it for another lesson."

He should have look dejected that I'd turned him down. Instead, his smile was radiant. He was so damned pleased with himself. "I'll hold you to it."

Justin

I couldn't stop staring at Kay. Smiling at Kay. Thinking about her. Thinking about having sex with her again. And again.

Her hair was finger-tousled and air-dried because her blow dryer was at my place. Practically no makeup. She'd used what she had in her purse. Which, to be honest, was practically a full makeup counter.

She wore a tank top, flip-flops, and pair of old shorts from college with the university logo on them. All her best stuff was at the penthouse. She was a little embarrassed. I was madly in love and too happy to think she looked anything other than hot.

I wore one of her old oversized college T-shirts the mascot had tossed to her at a football game.

"I used to wear this as a sleep shirt," she'd said when she tossed it to me. "This is a first for me, too. I've never given a guy a shacker shirt before." She laughed and clapped her hands, delighted. "I'm so going to love watching you do the Sunday morning walk of shame dressed in *my* clothes!"

She was a terrible tease, referring to college hookups like that.

I looked upward and shook my head, but I couldn't stop grinning. "You can't give your husband a shacker shirt. By definition, we didn't shack. We're married."

She laughed again. I loved her laugh. It made my whole day.

"Are we married? Really?" She gave me a pointed look and handed me a pair of men's black athletic shorts she dug out of one of her drawers. They might have been a pair Eric had left behind. I didn't ask. I didn't care.

"Yes, we are." I slipped on a pair of flip-flops she claimed her dad had forgotten at her place.

I hummed as we rode the elevator down to the lobby of her building, playing *Name That Tune* with Kay.

She shook her head and looked at me like I amused her. I'd take amused. For now.

"You have a nice humming voice." She sounded surprised.

When we reached the lobby, the light in the manager's office was on. The door stood open. I pulled Kay toward it.

She resisted. "What are you doing?"

I tugged her along. "Meeting the famous Carl," I whispered in her ear. "As you said, we need him on our side."

"It's Sunday. He won't be in."

I pointed. "His door's open."

"I hadn't noticed."

"You're hopeless," I said.

A big guy sat behind a desk, cursing at a computer screen.

Kay punched me playfully in the arm. I looked at her and mouthed, *What did I do?*

She called out to him, "Carl! What are you doing working on Sunday?"

He looked up, startled. "Kayla!" He stood and came forward to give her an exuberant hug. "I had a little work to catch up on." He looked me over with a critical eye. "This must be the new hubby."

I was grinning ear to ear. So damned happy I dared anyone to burst my bubble. As I stuck my hand out for a shake, he winked at me.

"You caught a good one." He slapped me on the back. "I protect all my tenants. You'd better treat her well." His tone was joking. But there was an edge to it, a hint of a threat. He, of all people, had something over on us.

"I intend to."

"Good." He gave me a thumbs-up.

I nodded toward his computer. "Having computer problems?"

"That damn thing is acting up." He explained the trouble.

I knew what the problem was. I could fix it in a matter of minutes. "Mind if I take a look? I'm pretty good with computers."

"I don't want to trouble you," he said. But his protest was feeble.

"No trouble at all." I took a seat in his chair and, in five computer strokes, fixed it. "There you go. We use this program, too. It's touchy. But I think you'll be okay now."

Carl thanked me. "You have to bring him around more often, Kayla. I could use a guy with his skills."

Kay looped her arm through mine. "Yes, he's brilliant with computers, isn't he?" She beamed at me.

I thought—I hoped, at least—that she really was proud.

The three of us chatted for a few minutes before we excused ourselves. Carl walked us to the door, inviting me back anytime.

"You impressed him," Kay whispered in my ear when we were out on the sidewalk.

"Yeah. That was the point. He's the one guy who could rat us out."

She nodded. "He won't. Especially now that you're his friend."

We left Kay's apartment building for her favorite café and bakery, hand in hand. I took full advantage of being in public and "acting." Out in the world, I didn't have to act uninterested in her. Mask my feelings. Or any of that other crap that made our private life complicated. I could smile fully, laugh wholly, and let the way I loved her shine in my eyes. It was a damnable situation for an introvert like me.

I was in the best mood of my life. I smiled at absolutely everyone we met. People smiled back with knowing looks, as if they knew I was a member of the club now. Every stoplight we came to was green. The sun was shining.

We got the last table, a two-topper in the prime location by the window, in the crowded bakery. The waitress was cute, friendly, and flirty. She laughed when I joked with her. When our coffee came, my latte had a heart made in the foamy milk on top. My chocolate chip muffin was loaded with chips and bigger than the rest of them in the display case. If I'd been alone, the waitress would have offered me her number.

Several other women in the bakery were eyeing me. The sexual confidence making love to Kayla had given me was astounding. And powerful. These women didn't appear to know who I was, were unaware of how much money I had, yet they wanted me.

Every sense of mine was heightened. My mind sharper than usual. The world was fresh and beautiful. It was sappy. And I'd never admit it to anyone, but Kay had just made my dreams come true.

It was also still true that she didn't love me. Yet. Dex had been right about that. But I was undeterred. I'd just proven we had the kind of earth-shattering chemistry you can't fake. Sex that powerful and awesome was rare and worth holding on to. All of that gave me a bigger start than I'd expected to have at this stage of the game.

Another thing, my random realization, added to my happiness—sex was messy. I couldn't say anything to Kay about it. But knowing what I knew now, unless the fake Kayla had taken time to scrub me down, there was no evidence of sex the next morning. And no evidence of cleanup, either. I could breathe a little easier. Not that I could prove we hadn't had sex. If it ever came to that. But the evidence was stronger and stronger that we hadn't.

Now, while Kay was flushed with the afterglow I'd given her, was the time to implement part two of the plan to keep her in my life.

CHAPTER FIVE

Kayla

Justin was simply unbelievable. He was glowing so brightly he was practically radioactive. He'd charmed Carl! It had taken me *months* to get Carl to warm up to me. Then again, I didn't have Justin's computer skills. On the walk to the café, he smiled, waved, and greeted people I'd seen every day for a year and never gotten a second look from. And our waitress, who was totally cute—the guys always noticed her—but usually harried and curt on busy mornings, brought him the best muffin in the case.

I stared at him. "Are you flirting with our waitress? Right in front of me, your adoring wife?"

He shrugged so casually it was almost comical. "Just being friendly. Jealous?"

"Oh, shut up, Mr. Sunshine, Haha I Finally Did the Deed." I sighed and muttered beneath my breath something about sleeping with a guy and turning him into Casanova. "She probably recognizes you and is expecting a huge tip, Mr. Billionaire."

His grin deepened, creasing his beard. "You *are* jealous." He leaned forward. "Don't worry. I'll give *you* a big tip later." He had the audacity to wink at me.

"Not if you keep flirting with everyone in the room, you won't." I lifted an eyebrow to let him know I was serious.

He laughed and took a bite of his muffin. Someone had left a section of the Sunday paper on the windowsill.

Jus picked it up and scanned it while he ate and sipped his coffee. His got a serious look on his face. He flipped the paper onto the table in front of me and pointed to an article, infographic included, about the philanthropic ventures of Seattle's local elite. Several EIEIO members were listed as some of the most generous people in the country, if not the world. The world's most generous man lived in Seattle, after all.

Jus flipped the paper onto the table and tapped it with his finger. "Riggins and I are trying to do something about this."

"You want to put a stop to philanthropy?" I said, deadpan.

He laughed. "Right, smartass. That's it. Death to all philanthropy." He rolled his eyes, which twinkled with amusement.

He was just so happy. I almost wanted to slap some sense in him.

I didn't know whether to be flattered or annoyed. And maybe, if I was honest, I was a bit annoyed because I realized I was pretty happy, too.

"We want to do our part," he said. "But we're novices at being billionaires. Well, I am. Riggins has a little more experience at being rich." Jus laughed. "I want you to meet him."

"I'd love to meet the mysterious Riggins." Which was absolutely true. I was insanely curious about Riggins. Who, like Lazer, had made the list of Seattle's most eligible rich guys many times over.

"He's not so mysterious. We'll get together with him soon." As Jus glanced at the paper again, a frown creased his forehead.

It could have just been me, but I thought it was exaggerated to impress me. Which was sweet of him.

"At Flash, we're trying to do our part to help the local community. All the proceeds from our sample sales go completely to community causes—battered women's shelters and the children's hospital. Volunteers from both organizations help organize the sales and man the cash registers at the events. Once a year, we have a huge sample sale and benefit that's open only to the patients, staff, and patrons of the hospital and domestic violence shelters we support. Our employees take over for the charities' volunteers."

"That's awesome." I took a bite of my filled croissant, getting powdered sugar on my lip and all over my fingers.

"Ophie's in charge of it." Jus made a dusting motion. "You have a little something..."

At the mention of Ophie's name, I sat up straighter, suddenly annoyed by the powdered sugar as I licked it off.

Okay, Ophie, I thought, feeling a little bit superior, but still unhappy at the thought of her. *I'm the one who made a man out of him. He's got my grin on his face. Why should I fear you?*

But I still didn't like the thought of her being in love with him.

Jus was watching me closely. "As the company has grown, so has the event. It's gotten out of hand. And frankly, it's too big a job for Ophie to handle. Especially with all her other job responsibilities."

He took my hand, squeezing it playfully. "I'd like you to be involved with Flash. I've offered before. I was serious about it. Now that we've gone public, it would be awkward for everyone if I hired you now."

"What are you thinking?" I said, trying not to get my hopes up.

"I'd like you to take the sample sales over from Ophie."

"Yes!" I couldn't hold my smile down. "I'm already bored staying home. A billionaire's wife can't just go out and get any old job. It just doesn't look good. And I've already called in rich at the one I had."

He nodded. "That's what I was thinking." He got an almost shy look on his face. "As a matter of fact, I was hoping you'd be game for taking over the bulk of my charitable obligations."

I frowned, unclear exactly what he was asking. "What do you mean? People are going to want to see *you* at events."

"I'm messing this up." He squeezed my hand. "I was thinking of starting a charitable foundation to oversee my charitable giving. We'd start small. The first task would be deciding which causes and charities to support. Besides the ones Flash already does. You could head it up. Help me get it started. Your first task will be the annual sample sale benefit."

Suddenly all the empty days in front of me were filled with exciting possibilities. My life had meaning. "Yes!" I said before he could change his mind.

He leaned across the table and kissed me. "Thanks, Kay. I really *do* need you."

His words, his tone, and the look in his eyes were so sincere, they hit me with a powerful force. I hadn't ever been needed that badly. And helping others in need would help me deal with the guilt of suddenly, undeservedly, being so filthy rich.

My mind filled with possibilities. Still, I hesitated. "I don't have a lot of experience. I was the philanthropy chair one year at my sorority. But that was it."

"That's okay," he said. "We'll start small. If you need help, we'll hire a manager with experience to guide you and run the day-to-day. Eventually, you'll be more the public face of it."

"What about in a year?" I fiddled with my napkin, tearing little bits of it off, suddenly nervous.

"We'll deal with that when it comes." He took a sip of coffee. "Which brings up another thing. Britt cornered me at the party. She wants a job at Flash. Given the circumstances, what do you think?"

I shrugged. Britt wanted the job so badly. "She'll be hurt if we don't give her a chance."

He nodded. "Yeah. There's no way out. Tell her to send me her résumé. I'll pass it along. I have to go through channels now, but I usually get my way." He paused. "It's going to be harder to keep up our game with her around the office all the time."

"You could always lowball her with your salary offer?" I said, and probably sounded way too hopeful.

"And get a bad rep for being a sweatshop?" He grimaced adorably.

I laughed.

Two attractive women about my age walked toward us, whispering to each other excitedly. They stopped at Justin's elbow.

The bolder one of them spoke. "Excuse us. Sorry to interrupt, but aren't you Justin Green, the owner of Flashionista?"

They were obviously nervous and impressed. And even though I was sitting right there, I was invisible to them as they tittered over him and flirted.

He nodded.

They just started gushing. "We love Flashionista! Over half my wardrobe and the stuff in my apartment is from your website. If it wasn't for Flash, I couldn't afford all the boutique stuff I have..."

On and on. They fell all over him.

Jus smiled, joked with them, was completely at ease and charming. He talked with them way too long, in my opinion. Could it be I was a tiny bit jealous of his attention being diverted?

I sat there mute, with a frozen smile hurting my face, until the waitress saved me by coming by to refill my coffee.

"Oh, sorry! We're taking up too much of your time," the bold one said, falling all over Jus.

"No. It's been great meeting you." Jus pulled his wallet out. "I love all our customers." He pulled two cards out of his wallet and handed one to each girl. "Gift cards. For your next order. To thank you for your loyalty."

The girls squealed happily, gave him flirty waves, and disappeared.

"How much did you give your fangirls?" I sounded grumpier than I meant to.

He shrugged. "Fifty apiece."

"Crap, Jus. Just for stroking your ego?"

He should have been mad. Instead, his smile deepened.

"You'd better give our waitress at least that," I said, still the grump. "If she hadn't moved them along, we'd be stuck here all day."

On Monday, I finally got a chance to go through that coat of Justin's where the mysterious letter was stashed. And it was...gone! Of course. Foiled again.

The producer of *Northwest Mornings*, a local Seattle morning TV show, called. She wanted to book me for an interview, the blushing new bride gushing over her billionaire groom. As more and more requests for interviews poured in, I began to contemplate getting an administrative or personal assistant for myself. Someone to manage my appointments and screen calls. The media had given us a few days off. A big news story about the current celebs of the moment had eclipsed my story of snagging the billionaire nerd boy. But the media frenzy from that had died down and I was news again.

I agreed to go on their Friday show. Now that I was taking over Justin and Flash's charitable work, I figured it would be a good place to announce it and get a jump on PR. I immediately booked several sessions with the top media coach in the city and began working on my public persona. Which, as far as I could tell, would be adoring wife and dedicated humanitarian. And, of course, fashionista dressed by Flashionista.

In my mind, I was playing out our year together. How soon until stories of our marriage sliding toward the rocks should appear? A few months before the end? A few weeks? What would our breakup look like? Could we part amicably, still friends?

I pushed thoughts of our parting away. There were growing increasingly depressing. Why should I think about them today when they could be pushed off to the distant future of a year?

Despite having fantastic sex together, and Jus adoring me and spoiling me completely and totally, he hadn't said he loved me. Not that I expected him to. I hadn't told him, either. Because I wasn't really in love with him. Not yet. But he was special to me, an intimate friend. And we had so much fun together.

First thing Monday morning, Jus set up a meeting between Ophie and me. She was too busy to meet with me until Wednesday. That was her claim, anyway. I believed she was putting me off in a pure power play. Frustrating. I couldn't publically announce my involvement in the charity sample sale until Ophie had been told and we'd met to discuss details and transitioning it to me.

In the meantime, I played alpha video game tester with Data on my lap. She was a good pup and seemed to enjoy the game, barking when I killed bad guys and made my way through the levels. Bonding with a dog over video games was interesting. It was so Justin to have a nerd dog.

My princess character was beautiful, and rather useless, as she floated along in the background. I made a note to complain to Lazer about that. In the meantime, I struck up an immediate online friendship with several other testers. Several, one in particular, were terrible flirts. But Lazer, despite his offer to play the game with me last Saturday, was never on when I was. And Jus declined to play, preferring to lock himself in his office and work on his Flashionista algorithms.

Wednesday was almost the longest day of the year. The merch girls at Flash got tired of waiting for an excuse to have a happy hour party to meet me. They planned a nearly shortest night of the year pub party, complete with karaoke, and issued Jus and me an invitation that couldn't be refused. Suddenly my Wednesday was booked—a coffee meeting with Ophie, followed by meetings with the top merch buyers, topped off by a hump day happy hour.

Wednesday afternoon, promptly at two, I met Jus and Ophie at a well-known local bakery near the Flash offices. It was crowded with tourists and office workers from downtown. Jus and Ophie were already there, working at a table in the corner, heads bent together intimately, laughing. It was clear from the familiarity between them they were used to working this way. In informal, date-like settings. At odd hours. I pictured them in the early days of Flash, working late together at the office. Or over candlelit dinners.

She poured Jus another cup of coffee from a small manual immersion brewer on the table. Ophie reached across him and dumped a packet of raw sugar into his cup, along with a splash of cream, like a long-married wife does for her husband. I'd seen my grandma do the same thing for Grandpa. Ophie even stirred the coffee for Jus. She knew, evidently, just how he liked his coffee. And anticipated his needs. I wondered if he was even aware of how she spoiled him.

I pushed down a bubble of jealousy.

Neither of them saw me come in. I got in line to get an iced coffee and one of the bakery's famous scones and watched them. How could Jus be drinking hot coffee on such a gorgeous, warm day? He drank entirely too much coffee, to be honest. And too many energy drinks as well. All that caffeine couldn't be good for him. I laughed at myself. Here I was worrying over him like an old hen. I wasn't his mom. Thank goodness.

When Ophie didn't think anyone was watching, her face shone with love and longing for Jus. He was clearly the sunshine in her day, so warm it scorched the rest of us. When he looked at her, she masked it. As well as she could. It was still a wonder to me that Jus didn't see it. Because as sure as the Seahawks were the city's favorite team, and destined to be Super Bowl champs again soon, everyone else in the bakery could.

I felt the sting of her desire for him as I waited in line. It bordered on obsession. And while that may have been flattering to Jus, it was dangerous to me. And us. And Flash. Not just because of the circumstances and Justin's crazy ID thief marriage we were covering up. Under any circumstance. She would put being close to Jus above Flash. Above everything. Even the law. I suppressed a shudder. And pushed away a premonition of darkness and trouble.

I was an intuitive person. I didn't discount my feelings of dread. Fear was a gift. That was what a book on self-defense I'd read said. Don't ever ignore it. And never, ever, underestimate your adversary. Especially when she wants your guy.

Ophie might seem meek and mild and geeky, matronly, definitely the underdog against glamour and fashion sense, but I wouldn't drop my guard. Her type run deep with unfulfilled passion. She struck me as exactly the kind who believed the end justified the means. For something she wanted.

Jus looked up as I finished paying for my scone and coffee. His face lit up when he saw me. He waved as the waitress handed me my white chocolate iced mocha.

I joined them at the table.

He stood and kissed me with pride of ownership and possession. And the absolute high of newfound sexuality. I would have said love, but that wasn't it. Maybe infatuation. Sex was still a shiny new toy for him and I was its vessel, his playground. A week ago, I would never have imagined he could be so confident. Did Ophie see the difference in him? Was she insanely jealous?

For the first time since Justin's sexual awakening, I felt like his mistress. A kept woman in every sense. Ophie and I were like two halves of what should have been one wife—a woman who adored and cared for him and a woman who gave him pleasure.

"Hey! You should have let me get that for you," he said as he held my chair out for me. He whispered in my ear, "You look beautiful." He sounded almost in awe.

He hadn't seen me since we'd tumbled around the bed together this morning. He left before I'd showered and dressed.

"Thank you." I stroked his bearded cheek and smiled at Ophie. "So good to see you again, Ophie. Thanks for making time to see me." It was hard to keep the sarcasm out of my voice.

"Jus tells me you're terribly busy. And now he's added more to your plate." I put just the right of amount of sympathy in my voice and on my face. "He says you're a wonder, a superhero of the office. I'm happy to be able to take the less pressing issues off your workload."

Yes, I was playing up to her. Praising her. Trying to put her off her guard. My words were sweet and soft. Feminine and totally guileless. In outward appearance only. In truth, they were totally calculated. And as barbed as the blooming blackberry bushes in every vacant lot in the city.

Jus had already told her he was moving the sample sales and charity events to me. If I had been anyone else, I imagined she would have been only too happy to off load that "fluffy" stuff. Though it wasn't fluffy at all. It was high profile, or would be in my hands. Good PR and advertising for Flash. Community goodwill was essential for any business to thrive. And Jus could use the goodwill, too. Always bank goodwill if you can.

Ophie nodded curtly. "Yes, good to see you, too. Jus has already explained the situation to me." She beamed at him.

Yes, beamed. Intentionally. To show me how close she was to him. Her chair was also indecently near his. Closer than mine. The way the table legs were positioned, it was impossible for me scoot any nearer to him. Without out-and-out sitting in his lap. And I hated the way she used the familiar of his name, Jus, like I did. It seemed unprofessional. Too friendly.

I had a vision of the future, of the two of them married, running Flash together. Of their children taking it over. I wondered if she *would* be successful at snagging him once our agreement ended and I let him go. She'd have to fight off and beat out a gaggle of hot girls. His newfound confidence would not be her ally.

The thought of them together made me irrationally sad and angry. A week ago, I had been semi-inclined to help her catch him. They seemed well suited in many areas. I would be walking away with my millions, so what would I care? As long as Jus was happy. But now? I wasn't so sure I would trust Jus to her.

"Ophie brought all the information you need. She knows everything. She's prepared to answer any and all questions." Jus beamed as he looked between us, his efficient admin and his trophy decoy wife.

Was he so completely unaware of the tension rippling between us, cold like the waters of Puget Sound sparkling outside our window? Or how much she disliked me and, as a consequence, I was growing to dislike her?

Jus got a text. He glanced at it. "Shit. There's a problem with the website. Tech needs me onsite immediately. I have to run. Sorry, Kay!" He squeezed my hand. "I'll see you later?"

I nodded. "Go!" The website was always top priority. "I'm meeting with some of the merch people after this. After work you and I can walk to the happy hour together."

"Excellent! Ophie can walk you back to Flash and get you checked in at reception." He slapped the table, took a last drink of his coffee, and gathered his things. "I'll leave you two to it!" He kissed me goodbye and was off.

Both Ophie and I watched him go. But I was watching her out of the corner of my eye. I hadn't been wrong. She was absolutely fixated on him.

When he was out of sight, she finally turned back to me and we got to work. She'd efficiently set me up with Flash's digital cloud and stored everything I needed there. I didn't know what made me think it, but I made a mental note to talk to Dex before I used my cloud account. And have him check for spyware. Dex was a computing genius, like Jus.

"The sample sales are a nightmare to stage," Ophie said. "The merch people are uncooperative, never committing to what will be in the sale until the last minute. Have you been to one of our sample sales?"

I shook my head. "Never had the pleasure. I haven't been either a friend or family long." No, I couldn't resist getting in that subtle show of my superior position. She may have been an employee. But I was family, first family, of Flash now.

"I've heard they're wild. People scrambling for treasures. Pawing through boxes. Like a huge garage sale on steroids." I couldn't keep my excitement at the thought of a sample sale out of my voice. Who didn't love a hotly contested race for the best bargains at a sample sale?

Ophie gently lifted one eyebrow, clearly not pleased with my description of the delightful mayhem. Like I'd offended her.

"Yes, well. Keeping the sales organized and under control is like trying to herd cats. We group items by category and size. But within minutes, everything's a mess." She went on to elaborate the trials of running a sample sale.

It was clear the merch people, with their interest in fashion and style, with their foreign creative thought processes and right-brained activity, weren't her kind of people. She didn't relate to them. Nor they to her. I didn't anticipate having that kind of problem.

We were winding down when my phone rang. Ophie waved at me impatiently, in that dismissive way. "Go ahead and take your call." She began clearing our plates and cups.

I glanced at my phone and my heart flipped. "Lazer!"

"Hey, princess."

"Princess, indeed! Like you would know. You've been suspiciously absent online lately."

"I've been online. Just not when you are, apparently. And sadly." He laughed. "I'll be on tonight. Around ten. If you're available, ask Jus to join us. We'll make it a threesome."

I laughed. A threesome, indeed.

Ophie pretended disinterest, but was eavesdropping, clearly.

I turned my back to her as I scooped up my things. "To what do I owe the pleasure of this call?"

"I'm calling with an offer of help. Jus tells me you're taking over his philanthropic arm, particularly that monster of a sample sale and the annual gala. I have a wonderful, efficient admin intern whose services I'd like to offer. Free of charge. Think of it as a charitable donation. She has a heart for charitable work and is looking to enter the non-profit sector when she finishes her MBA. Taking her on would be a favor to both of us.

"She's so efficient, I'm having a hard time keeping her busy enough. She has experience with charities and fundraising. Can you use her for a few months until she heads back to school?"

"You must have read my mind. I was just thinking I need an assistant."

"Good. Let's arrange for you to meet her. If you like her, she's yours. For a while, at least."

"Excellent." I hesitated. "Lazer, I wanted to tell you how much I love my character." And wished she wasn't such a damsel in distress. "Will she be part of the public release of the game?"

"Absolutely!"

Ha! I thought. *Jus and his silly theories.*

When I glanced over my shoulder, I didn't like the way Ophie was looking at me. Like I was a specimen in a jar, one whose wings were about to be pinned.

I walked the three blocks back to the office with Ophie. She was amazingly chipper. Which put me on edge. Just what did she suddenly think she had up on me? At the office, she introduced me to the receptionist, got me a visitor's badge, and grudgingly dropped me off at Justin's door. Earlier, he'd insisted he be the one to show me around.

"Website's up and running like it should be again. But I only have a few minutes." He looked harried, but beaming. "I'll have to give you the quick version of the tour on the way to Marla's office. Sorry, babe. I'll give you a more thorough tour another time."

Look at the way he called me babe. Wasn't he adorable?

I stared out at the view from his office in awe. "No wonder you don't want to come home. This view is better than the penthouse's!"

He laughed. "If you like mountains." He was staring at me. "The view from in here is pretty damn good." He took my arm. "Come on. Let me introduce you to Riggins first. His office is next door."

Unfortunately, Riggins was out.

"You'll meet him at the happy hour tonight." Jus took me by the elbow and gave me the five-minute tour, showing me off with obvious husbandly pride to everyone we met. And equally, showing Flashionista off with the proud manner of a founding father.

The Flash offices were a dream come true to someone like me. The photography department was full of backdrops, props, and cutting-edge fashion and clothes, clothes, clothes! Plus accessories galore. Complete and utter heaven.

He introduced me to Barry, the head of facilities, Wylie, head of operations, and finally dropped me off at the office of the head buyer, Marla.

We hit it off immediately. She was older than I was, but we quickly discovered common ground. We'd both graduated from the same university. We immediately broke into stories of the professors we'd had and the stunts we'd pulled.

"We have quite a few alum here. I'll introduce you," she said.

It turned out there were more than a few. I had nearly a dozen fellow former classmates working at Flash. I met at least a half-dozen more senior merch buyers who were in charge of categories. After the initial awkwardness over me being the boss' wife, the formality and standoffishness quickly wore off. We were soon laughing and joking. I was high on the feeling of being surrounded by so many like-minded people. It felt like being back in the sisterhood. These were my peeps.

Ideas about the sample sale and event flew at the speed of sound. I had no idea why Ophie had so much trouble with the buyers. If she'd only not looked down her nose at them as her intellectual inferiors...

The merch buyers explained the decision process used to determine what went into the sale, how they contacted the suppliers, and the reasons why some samples were in doubt until the last minute.

Just before five, I got a text from Jus saying he was running late. What a shock. Ha! I was impressed that he was actually going to try to leave by five.

The girls invited me to come along with them to the bar. I texted Jus that I'd meet him there.

At the bar, I settled into a large booth with three of my former classmates and two new girls. I ordered a lemon drop, because what was better on a hot summer day than a cool lemon drink rimmed with sugar?

Now that we were out of the office, the conversation turned personal.

"I can't believe you married Justin Green!" my former classmate Sarah said.

Yes, I'd expected this line of conversation. I opened my mouth to respond with the usual *But he's changed so much—*

"He's absolutely the most completely adorable billionaire anywhere! I dare you to find another one like him in the whole wide world. You're so *incredibly* lucky." Sarah leaned forward on her elbows toward me. "Any of us would have loved to bed that boy! And marry him? Wow! That was the ultimate fantasy. How did you do it?"

I shrugged, dumbfounded. Had Sarah not known Jus in college? Had his growth spurt and bearded transformation happened before he started Flash? Had he banished that awkward, nerdy behavior and nervousness around girls so quickly after college?

The rest of the girls leaned forward with her, cooing their agreement.

"He was sweetly scruffy before," one of the girls said. "Now that you've obviously fixed him up, he's absolutely delectable. Totally hot in that hip Seattle way. He has the vibe."

"Tell us your secret!" the girl on my right said.

The conversation flew, bouncing around the table so rapidly it was hard to keep track of the speakers.

"One of us can still land a billionaire. Riggins is single. The dream remains alive until the last billionaire is wed."

"Or dead."

The girls laughed.

"I don't know," another said. "He's so much less approachable than Justin."

"Way more *GQ*, you mean."

"And sophisticated."

"Justin was the catch, I admit it. There's something sweet and attainable about him."

"And yet killer," the blond new girl said. "He can definitely take out the competition. In fact, he has. Remember how he shut down that competing startup? His algorithms blew them out of the water."

"There's also something sexy about a brainy guy." The other new girl sighed. "Especially when he's hot and he doesn't know it."

"Justin is always so nice to us. Remember when he invented buyer's day and took us all out to lunch and gave us each a bouquet of flowers he picked up at the market?"

Another girl nodded. "Yes, but that was back when Flash was so much smaller. A fourth its current size. Still, what boss does that? And that was *before* the IPO, which is really what made him rich."

"Used his own money, too, not company money."

"And he started the sample sales just for us," the buyer whose name I kept getting mixed up said. Courtney? "Just before Christmas so we could all buy fabulous presents for everyone. Our salaries were crap at the time. I got my mom a necklace and sweater worth hundreds for under ten dollars. That was three years ago. She still wears them and brags about the compliments she gets on them."

"And he always comes to happy hour when he can. And buys a round of drinks."

"And sings karaoke like a good sport."

Five heads nodded.

Sarah took charge again. "So? How'd you do it, Kayla? What's your secret?"

Five pairs of eyes stared at me with admiration and the hope that I would impart the secret formula for bedding a billionaire.

I was dizzy from the bouncing conversation. "Get them drunk?" I made a face and shrugged.

The girls all laughed like I was kidding.

"Well, that's easy enough," Sarah said. "Especially here! But it can't be the whole truth. We've tried to ply Justin with booze before and come up empty-handed. Give us the details. Spill your love story!"

I fed them the approved story, trying to make it sound as romantic as possible. Which it wasn't, of course. How do you make the romance of the century out of two college acquaintances meeting up again, getting hammered, and tying the knot?

"Hmmmm..." Sarah pulled her mouth to one side. "The secret seems to be getting sent on business to the Reno fulfillment center. A city where quickie weddings can easily be performed twenty-four seven. And *then* getting them drunk. And wed."

"Exactly," I said, feeling mellow from my lemon drop.

Everyone laughed.

"So now we just have to get Riggins to take one of us to Reno on business. Easy, right? Should we draw straws to see who gets the honor?"

"Yeah, but Riggins isn't an easy mark. He holds his alcohol too well."

"And he likes the expensive stuff. The stuff out of range of our budgets."

"Unless he's buying!"

They nodded in unison, like a dance troupe or a group of Sea Gals. Just then Jus walked in the door next to a tall, immaculately groomed guy with a delicious head of hair, who was wearing the latest, trendiest in men's summer fashion. I knew in an instant I must be looking at Riggins in the flesh. His pictures didn't do him justice. He oozed charisma, if that was possible. Next to him, Jus just looked...young.

When Jus spotted me, his face lit up, transforming him. He waved and came toward us with Riggins in tow.

"Well, aren't *we* lucky?" Sarah whispered. "Here they come." She sighed as she eyed Riggins. "We'll all be hanging with you from now on, Kayla. You're our new bestie."

The men stopped in front of our booth. I was on the end. I slid out and kissed Jus, to mark him as mine as much as for show.

I hadn't realized just quite how well loved and loved to be loved he was. Once he ditched me, he would have no problem finding a new mate among his staff. Maybe I should even pick her out and throw him her direction. Anything to keep him from Ophie. My stomach tightened at the thought. There was that little green monster again. Selfish, *selfish*.

Jus introduced me to Riggins, who was polite and pleasant, but slightly aloof. Maybe he was just hard to get to know. I remembered the girls saying he was less approachable than Jus. But I thought it was more than that. He was evaluating me. Taking my stock as if his stock in Flash depended on it. Which it did. But he couldn't know how much.

Still, I supposed he wasn't wild about Jus marrying on the spur of a drunken moment. With presumably no prenup. To someone who could be a gold-digging woman who ended up with half of Justin's part of the company in a nasty divorce. And accompanying media blitz. When I put it like that, no wonder he was leery.

Riggins didn't know about the ironclad postnup, obviously. And I couldn't reassure him. We'd just have to tiptoe around each other until he grew to trust me. Or maybe until I left in a year with "only" ten million of Justin's pocket change.

The bar quickly filled with Flash employees getting off shift. Riggins, flashing his enigmatic *GQ* smile, ordered a round of drinks for everyone on him. And made an elegant, thoughtful toast to us.

Jus introduced me to more and more staffers until I was completely overwhelmed with names and titles and job descriptions and personal details. The way Jus knew every employee's name was impressive. And so personal. He treated each employee, no matter how new and lowly, as if they mattered to him and were an old friend.

He asked them about their assignments and whether they were happy. He asked about their families and their pets. He remembered intricate details of their lives, as if each one was one of his closest friends. I realized then it wasn't at all surprising he knew, and remembered, so much about my parents and their home. I shouldn't have been either creeped out or flattered. That was just Jus being Jus. And so were the flowers he'd sent ahead. And the champagne.

I was swept away from my merch buyer friends and ended up at a bar-height table near the karaoke stage, sitting between Riggins and Jus. Jus held my hand in one hand and a beer in the other. The bar was noisy and loud. I was trying to hear something Riggins was saying when a chant went up for karaoke to commence.

And then, like two good sports, Riggins and Jus excused themselves to take the stage.

Riggins took the mic. "My buddy Jus and I usually kick the night off with one of our classic duets."

"I don't know if classic quite describes them!" someone heckled.

Riggins ignored it. "But tonight Jus has asked to open the night with a solo. So, Jus, my man, take it away." He slapped Jus on the back and took his seat next to me.

Jus cleared his throat. "This one's for my bride. She hasn't been to one of these before—"

"She's in for a treat," one of the guys called out.

"So go easy on her," Jus said with a grin. "And me. And if you don't like the music selection, don't blame me. It's eighties night tonight." He turned to the DJ. "Maestro?"

And then he broke into a round of "You Make My Dreams Come True" by Hall and Oates, singing just to me. Although the song had come out before I was born, I knew it from the oldies station Mom listened to. And that movie *500 Days of Summer.* Which was the best breakup movie, *ever.* I should know. I'd watched it after every breakup with Eric. Including the last one.

Thinking about my inevitable breakup with Jus, I got a lump in my throat. But this song was from the scene where the hero, Tom, is madly in love with Summer. It was so upbeat, you couldn't help dancing along to it in your seat. At least tap your feet.

Justin jumped around, mimicking the dancing in the movie, badly. But he was still cute. Even though his moves needed work and would scare off the bluebird of happiness before it landed on his finger, like it did on Tom's.

But Justin's voice! *His voice.* Deep and true and beautiful. Toe-curling sexy. Penetrating to the soul. Fun and filled with joy and good humor. His eyes sparkled. His smile was brilliant. He was having the time of his life up there. I didn't know why I should have been so surprised. His speaking voice was to die for. And his humming voice pleasant and on key.

I caught a glimpse of Ophie in the crowd. She was sitting at a table on the perimeter of the stage. She had a look of rapture on her face while Jus sang. I could only imagine how much she roiled inside knowing he was singing to me.

He pointed to me as he sang and danced, if you could call it that, to the table. He took my hand and pulled me onto the stage with him so he could look deep into my eyes as he sang. The crowd of his employees ate it up. There's nothing like seeing the boss make a fool of himself on stage and in love.

I loved dancing. I'd taken years of lessons. So I played along, moving with the song while he sang. Even wrapping myself around him when the lyrics called for it.

His employees loved it, clapping and bouncing to the upbeat song about, well, a girl making a guy's dreams come true. Duh.

When the song ended, Jus pulled me into a kiss. The crowd erupted in applause. Riggins, Wylie, and four other guys came up on stage. And then, in another movie moment, the seven guys broke into an a cappella version of the theme song from the eighties movie *The Breakfast Club*, "Don't You (Forget About Me)," with me at the center like they were all wooing me.

They were wonderful. The moment was perfect. I was breathless and happier than I could have imagined.

The door to the bar opened. A noisy group of guys tumbled in. I looked over at them just as the tall, good-looking jock of the group locked gazes with me.

Eric.

Crap. There went my perfect moment.

Gina Robinson is the award-winning author of the contemporary new adult romances *Rushed*, *Crushed*, *Reckless Longing*, *Reckless Secrets*, and *Reckless Together* and the Agent Ex series of humorous romantic suspense novels. She's currently working on the next installment of Switched at Marriage.

Connect with Gina Online:

My Website: http://www.ginarobinson.com/
Twitter: @ginamrobinson
Facebook: www.facebook.com/GinaRobinsonAuthor

www.ingramcontent.com/pod-product-compliance
Lightning Source LLC
Chambersburg PA
CBHW071627140626
46555CB00021B/970